Journeys Into Alternate Realities

FOUR SCIENCE FICTION SHORT STORIES

BARNABAS TIBURTIUS

CONTENTS

DECLARATION

At the outset, the author would like to declare that while the places and geographical locations referenced within this work may be factual, all characters and names are entirely fictional and do not identify any real individuals. Any resemblance to actual people, living or dead, is purely coincidental.

The narrative interlocks real and imagined elements to create a scenario that stimulates the reader's imagination while drawing on the rich context of authentic settings. While certain events may be inspired by true occurrences or reflect societal issues, the portrayal of these elements is intended for artistic expression rather than historical accuracy.

Additionally, specific data, statistics, and information presented in the text have been thoroughly researched and deemed valid at the time of writing. The author acknowledges the fluidity of facts and encourages readers to seek further knowledge about the topics explored. This work aims to provoke thought and evoke emotion while navigating the tenuous line between reality and fiction.

Thank you for embarking on this journey where the real and the imagined coexist.

ACKNOWLEDGEMENTS

As I pen the final words of this book, I am drawn to reflect on the remarkable journey that brought these stories to life, a journey spanning three decades, enriched by the wisdom of ancient mythologies and the subtleties of human consciousness. This book owes its existence to countless inspirations and the unwavering support of those who have accompanied me on this path.

First and foremost, I extend my deepest gratitude to my wife, whose companionship has illuminated the countless miles travelled across Europe. Your unwavering support, patience, and enthusiasm have been my constant north star. Our shared explorations through the hauntingly beautiful landscapes of the United Kingdom have gifted us memories as vivid and enduring as the stories themselves.

To our daughter, Anne, and son-in-law, Graham Day: your insightful guidance and passionate encouragement have been invaluable. Your keen perspectives and dedication to facilitating my research journeys have enabled me to delve deeper into the rich histories that form the backdrop of these tales. Thank you for being pillars of support and wisdom.

This collection is deeply rooted in the expansive fields of Sumerian, Egyptian, and Indian mythologies. I owe a debt of gratitude to the scholars and storytellers who have spent their lives illuminating these ancient worlds. Their work has been instrumental in shaping my understanding and inspiring the mythological frameworks within my stories.

Furthermore, I express my admiration and appreciation to the pioneers of consciousness studies, especially in the realm of panpsychism. Their groundbreaking research has opened pathways of thought that challenged and expanded my understanding of the mind and its intricate relationship with reality. This book is a testament to the endless possibilities that arise when ancient wisdom meets cutting-edge ideas.

The enigmatic realms of quantum reality and cosmology have profoundly influenced these narratives. My sincere gratitude to the scientific community, whose explorations of the cosmos have provided stunning insights into the nature of existence. Their work has fueled my imagination, allowing me to draw connections between the cosmic and the conscious in ways that enrich the scenario of these stories.

The insights into Jungian psychology, too, have been instrumental in shaping the characters and themes within this collection. I am indebted to the legacy of Carl Jung and the psychologists who continue to expand on his work, exploring the depths of the human psyche with courage and intellect.

Lastly, I wish to acknowledge the authors, past and present, whose works have ignited my imagination and offered new paradigms from which to view the world. While this book aspires to originality, it is built upon the storytelling traditions that have come before it. Thank you to those storytellers whose whispers echo through these pages.

To all these individuals and communities who have enriched my life and work, I extend my heartfelt thanks. This book is a collaborative scenario, and it is my hope that it resonates with readers as a testament to the power of narrative to transcend time, culture, and reality.

Finally, the credit is due to 'STOCKCAKE IMAGES' for the cover image, Attribution to: Photo by Photo by <a href="https://stockcake.com/i/cosmic-mirror-portal_20645 25_1248158">Stockcake</a>

PREFACE

In the labyrinthine scenario of human experience, stories serve as both threads and weavers, binding the known to the unknown, the seen to the unseen. My journey towards compiling this collection of paranormal stories spans over three decades—a pilgrimage of sorts, through the nooks and crevices of ancient mythologies, the quantum dance of reality, the vast expanses of cosmology, and the intricate layers of psychology. This compendium invites readers to step beyond the ordinary, into realms where the occult and the metaphysical intermingle, creating a scenario woven from the enigmas of myth and the vast potentialities of the human mind.

For thirty years, Europe—particularly the evocative landscapes and haunted histories of the United Kingdom—has been my canvas and my muse. Through my extensive travels across these lands, I have encountered tales steeped in folklore, whispers of the past that echo in the present. England and Scotland, with their ancient ruins, mist-covered moors, and storied castles, offer a unique theatre for such narratives. It is a place where history and mystery fuse, where every shadow may harbor a story waiting to be told.

I have sought to infuse these stories with an authenticity that honors the rich traditions and landscapes from which they spring. Yet, in crafting these tales, I also draw upon a myriad of influences, both contemporary and timeless.

The quasi-reality in which these stories unfold mirrors the delicate balance between myth and reality space where the imagination shapes and is shaped by the echoes of past masters in the art of storytelling.

These stories do not merely borrow from folklore or earlier works but aspire to transcend their origins, synthesizing the ageless with the modern in a narrative dance that recognizes no boundaries. Each story is a prism, reflecting myriad hues of human emotion and experience. They challenge our perceptions of reality, blurring the lines between the conscious and the subconscious, the material and the ethereal.

In exploring the supernatural, I delve into the very fibers of human consciousness as uncharted as any ghostly apparition or mythical creature. Here, I engage with the latest insights from quantum physics, where reality itself is made of threads as mysterious as those in our most ancient myths. This intersection of advanced science and ancient wisdom serves as the underpinning of these stories, offering readers a journey not just across continents but across the dimensions of thought and being.

Moreover, the cosmological themes are integral to the essence of these stories. The cosmos, with its unfathomable mysteries and infinite expanses, mirrors the depths of the human psyche and the limitless horizon of human imagination. In exploring the paranormal, we are, in essence, gazing into the cosmic mirror, challenging our understanding of life, death, and everything in between. It is this profound connection between the mind and the cosmos that brings depth to these narratives, inviting readers to embark on a voyage beyond the stars, where possibilities are boundless, and every shadow holds a promise of discovery.

Psychology, too, plays a vital role in this collection. The human mind is a fertile ground for the paranormal, a labyrinth where fear and fascination coexist. By delving into the psychological dimensions, these stories explore the deepest fears and highest aspirations of our shared humanity. They reflect the complexities and contradictions of the human spirit, revealing the shadows that lurk in the corners of our consciousness and the lights that guide us through the darkness.

To the best of my knowledge and efforts, I believe these fictions to be original in their entirety and approach. Each story in this collection stands as a unique testament to a passion for the paranormal and a commitment to the art of storytelling. While they might echo the creations and frameworks of others who have walked similar paths, I hope these stories resonate with readers through their authenticity and originality, sparking curiosity, wonder, and reflection.

As you turn the pages of this book, I invite you to journey with me into the realms of the uncanny and the extraordinary. Whether you are a curious sceptic, an intrepid seeker of the supernatural, or a lover of finely spun tales, these narratives offer an explorational map to a world where reality bends, shadows speak, and the impossible becomes possible.

Welcome, then, to the world of the paranormal place where every story is a thread weaving the fabric of our shared quest through the unknown. May this collection inspire, entertain, and transport you, as it has for me, on a timeless journey through the landscapes of myth and the uncharted territories of the human mind.

Barnabas Tiburtius,

Chennai,

April 2025

WHISPERS OF HARLOWE MANOR

Jeremy Kiln was born and raised in the vibrant, if chaotic, heart of London. His childhood was spent in a modest flat above his father's repair shop, where the clanging of tools mingled with the distant hum of city life. His mother, an avid reader and part-time librarian, nurtured his early love for stories, often regaling him with tales from classic literature and the latest mystery novels. It was in these formative years that Jeremy developed an unyielding curiosity, a desire to understand the world around him in all its complexities.

Jeremy pursued journalism at university, driven by a passion for uncovering the truth and telling stories that might otherwise remain hidden. Early in his career, he wrote for a local paper, tackling stories that showcased human interest and societal issues. His investigative pieces soon caught the attention of larger publications, eventually leading him to cover international stories. Over time, Jeremy grew hyper-focused on tangible evidence, developing a journalistic philosophy that prized facts over conjecture. Witnessing the darker facets of humanity instilled a scepticism that became a defining aspect of his personality.

Throughout his career, Jeremy achieved recognition for his work, collecting awards for pieces that highlighted issues ranging from corruption to human rights abuses. However, the demands of his profession and his relentless pursuit of truth gradually created a rift between him and those around him. Personal relationships faltered; friends faded into distant contacts, and romantic connections fizzled out, leaving Jeremy somewhat isolated.

His assignments took him to war zones and disaster sites, locations teeming with peril and stories waiting to be unravelled. It was this high-stakes environment that cemented his reputation as a tenacious, if not overly sceptical, journalist. Yet, beneath his professional accolades lay a restlessness born from the relentless cycle of uncovering grim truths without touching on deeper, more personal stories of redemption or transformation.

When approached to investigate Harlowe Manor—a site rumoured to be steeped in mystery and supernatural phenomena—Jeremy viewed it as an opportunity to step out of the ordinary grind of journalism. Despite his scepticism toward the paranormal, he was intrigued by the challenge of separating myth from reality, hoping to explore the human stories hidden within the layers of legend.

Jeremy first heard about Harlowe Manor through a colleague at the newspaper where he worked. The manor had become a point of interest recently due to claims by paranormal enthusiasts and local historians alike, suggesting it was more than just a dilapidated old building. Ghost hunters had reported unusual electromagnetic readings, and others spoke of strange apparitions visible only at the corners of their eyes.

While Jeremy was sceptical, his editor believed that a fresh take on a classic ghost story could captivate their audience. He was tasked with writing a feature article that dug into both the myths and the realities surrounding the manor. However, his editor wanted a new angle—something that could blend the human-interest story with the deep, potentially existential questions about life and death.

Jeremy was a man driven by curiosity and a relentless pursuit of truth. His career in journalism had taken him to the furthest reaches of the world where he encountered humanity at its rawest. Scarred by both disappointments and triumphs, Jeremy approached each new assignment with a mixture of scepticism and hope. Over the years, he had developed an uncanny knack for sniffing out stories, a skill that had made him both respected and occasionally feared among his peers.

During a preliminary gathering of information, one particular name kept surfacing: Dr. Emily Sloane. She had recently published an article on near-death experiences and the potential for residual human energy within psychically charged locations like Harlowe Manor. Her work had gained attention for its unique blend of scientific rigour and openness to the supernatural.

Dr. Emily Sloane grew up in the coastal town of Brighton, where the calming rhythm of the sea influenced her inquisitive nature. From a young age, she was fascinated by the human mind, leading her to pursue psychology. Studying at a prestigious university, Emily focused on the intersection of consciousness and the unexplained, particularly near-death experiences—a field that sparked both controversy and interest.

Emily became known for her pioneering research into the phenomena of consciousness at the threshold of life and death. Her work questioned conventional boundaries, delving into subjects like soul transmigration and karmic influences that conventional psychology often avoided. She published articles in both academic journals and popular science magazines, aiming to demystify experiences often dismissed as mere psychological anomalies. Her open-minded approach drew interest and scepticism alike, painting her as a brilliant yet somewhat unconventional scholar.

Emily's interest in the subject was deeply personal. As a child, she had a profound, otherworldly experience that defied explanation—a brush with danger that left her questioning the nature of existence. This event became the impetus for her perennial quest to understand what lies beyond our immediate perception of reality. Her professional journey was not just about academic inquiry but also about seeking answers to questions that had haunted her since childhood.

Emily, on the other hand, was a seeker in her own right, though her pursuit lay in the realms of the mind and soul. A blend of academic brilliance and intuitive understanding had propelled her into leading conversations about the nature of consciousness and the afterlife. Her theory—those souls carried karmic imprints affecting each subsequent life—had been dismissed by sceptics but embraced by forward-thinking circles. Harlowe Manor was to be a proving ground, a place where she hoped the past and present would converge in shared revelation.

Jeremy reached out to Dr. Sloane through a mutual connection—a fellow journalist who had interviewed her for an article on consciousness and science. Initially, Emily was cautious. As a scientist, she was familiar with the sometimes-sensationalistic reporting in her field, wary of being misrepresented. However, intrigued by Jeremy's reputable background and his intent to approach the story with nuance, she agreed to a meeting.

They first met at a bustling café in central London. Jeremy was seated at a quiet corner table, sifting through his notes when Emily arrived. Her presence was immediately engaging—sharp eyes behind frameless glasses, her demeanour both thoughtful and approachable.

Their conversation unfolded over several hours, during which Jeremy outlined his assignment, emphasising his desire to humanise the narrative rather than exploit the sensational aspects. Emily, in turn, spoke passionately about her research and the unexplored dimensions of consciousness that might play out in a place like Harlowe Manor.

"What fascinates me about Harlowe," Emily explained, "is the interplay between the historical narrative and personal experiences reported over the decades. My work suggests that locations like these are imprinted with human emotions and energies—residues of lives once lived. I'd like to see if there's a scientific basis we could explore together."

Jeremy appreciated her analytical yet open-minded approach. For him, Emily provided a perfect counterbalance—an ally who could lend authority and depth to the exploration of the unknown. He was intrigued by her scientific validation of concepts he was more inclined to dismiss but was also eager to learn from her unique perspective.

Realising their combined skills—his investigative eye and her scientific insight—could offer a comprehensive examination of Harlowe Manor, they agreed to collaborate. Jeremy's task would be storytelling, capturing the heart of what they would uncover, while Emily would spearhead the analysis of any phenomena they might encounter, grounding their findings in her research field.

As they planned their approach, both felt a growing sense of anticipation, aware that this project might not only enrich their professional lives but also challenge their personal views on reality. Thus, what began as a professional collaboration quickly promised to be a profound journey of understanding, blending Jeremy's search for truth with Emily's exploration of the soul's mysteries.

The partnership was set up, each bringing their strengths to the table as they prepared to confront the many layers of history and mystery within the walls of Harlowe Manor.

The assignment at Harlowe Manor offered Emily an opportunity to explore a world entwined with her academic theories, alongside a journalist known for uncovering truths. The collaboration with Jeremy posed a personal challenge and an intellectual delight. Emily was keen to approach the manor's mysteries through both scientific inquiry and imaginative exploration.

The narrow road twisted through the Sussex countryside, lined with ancient oaks whose gnarled branches clawed at the overcast sky. The late afternoon sun struggled to pierce the thick canopy of clouds, casting a muted silver glow over the desolate landscape. As the car progressed along the winding path, fields of wild, untamed grasses stretched out on either side, their stalks whispering secrets in the wind.

Jeremy gripped the steering wheel with tense fingers, casting a sidelong glance at the sprawling countryside. In his years as a journalist, he had chased countless stories through bustling cities and remote outposts alike, but this place—Harlowe Manor—held an ominous allure that both intrigued and unsettled him. The navigation system on the dashboard blinked uncertainly as if reluctant to draw any closer to their destination.

Beside him, Emily absently traced patterns in the window, her mind working through theories and histories that danced on the edge of reason. A psychologist by trade, her fascination with near-death experiences had recently led her down more unconventional paths. Her latest research promised revelations about the transmigration of souls, and she believed that Harlowe Manor might just hold the key.

"Almost there," Jeremy spoke up, his voice breaking through the quiet hum of the engine. "Are you ready for this?"

Emily slowly turned away from the window, her eyes glowing with fervent excitement that was intricately woven with a thread of apprehension. It was the kind of anxious anticipation one feels when standing on the precipice of the unknown, the boundary where curiosity dances with uncertainty. "As prepared as anyone might be when stepping into the enigmatic abyss," she declared with a steady, determined voice, despite the subtle tremor of fear that lingered beneath. Her thoughts seemed to intertwine with the hidden secrets of the place, stories that whispered chilling tales of its mysteries, beckoning her forward while cautioning restraint.

Jeremy nodded, considering the tales of haunting and cursing that surrounded the manor. Yet, beyond the allure of the supernatural, there was a promise of uncovering something profoundly human—a glimpse into the lives and struggles of those long pasts. That was what drew him: the story yet untold.

As the dense foliage reluctantly surrendered to the narrow, winding path, Jeremy and Emily found themselves transfixed by the scene unfolding before them. The air was thick with an otherworldly presence, as if time itself held its breath. At the hill's crest, Harlowe Manor emerged like a spectral sentinel, its solemn grandeur painted starkly against the brooding twilight sky. The manor, wrapped in an eerie luminescence, appeared almost alive, its ancient stones whispering secrets long forgotten. Shadows raced across the façade, dancing with a life of their own, while the windows glimmered with an unsettling anticipation, resembling eyes that watched from a realm beyond. The wind carried an unsettling symphony of distant whispers, hints of past tragedies echoing around them. Vines, gnarled and twisting like skeletal fingers, clung to the manor's walls, further accentuating its aura of haunting beauty. Each step they took up the path seemed heavier, burdened by the palpable energy that radiated from the manor. The air grew colder, chilling them to the bone, as they drew nearer to this mysterious apparition that both beckoned and warned. They knew they were not just approaching a building, but rather a gateway to the unknown, filled with haunting promises of what lay beyond.

Harlowe Manor was a monument to bygone opulence, caught in the relentless creep of decay. Constructed in the 19th century, its architecture was a blend of Gothic Revival and Victorian eccentricity. Spires and gables reached skyward, while intricate stonework hinted at the prosperity and ambition of its original builders.

The façade was mottled with age, the once-vibrant red brick now dulled and crumbling in places. Ivy crept up the walls in tangled patterns, embracing the structure as if seeking to reclaim it entirely. Tall, narrow windows lined the manor's front, their panes reflecting glimpses of the grey sky like distant memories trapped within.

The drive circled around a neglected fountain at the entrance, its once-proud centrepiece now softened with moss and neglect. Jeremy parked the car with a slight sense of reverence, aware of the weight of history pressing down around them.

Emily stepped out, the chill in the air seeping through her coat. She took in the manor's imposing presence, both awed and uneasy about what lay inside.

As they approached the oak door, Jeremy couldn't shake the feeling of being watched. His imagination conjured images of long-gone residents peering from the windows, curious about these newcomers disturbing their eternal slumber. He drew a deep breath, reminding himself that while he had faced many challenges, the stories were still just stories—until proven otherwise.

Emily paused to take in the atmosphere, an electric anticipation thrumming beneath her scientific curiosity. "If walls could talk," she mused softly. To her, the manor was more than bricks and mortar—it was a repository of energy, the souls of its past inhabitants echoing their joys and sorrows, waiting to be understood. Internal monologues traced their thoughts as they stood.

After settling in at the manor, Jeremy and Emily decided to visit the nearby village to gather more context for their investigation. The village of Ashcombe, nestled in a valley surrounded by rolling hills, was a quaint assortment of cobblestone streets and timbered cottages that appeared untouched by time.

They arrived at The Grey Swan, a bustling pub and the focal point of village social life. Inside, the air was thick with the aroma of roasting meat and ale. Locals congregated in small groups, exchanging stories in low, conspiratorial tones.

As Jeremy and Emily approached the bar, conversation hushed momentarily, a palpable tension filling the room.

"My name's Jeremy, and this is Dr Emily Sloane," Jeremy introduced them with a cordial smile. "We're staying at Harlowe Manor for a short while." A murmur spread through the patrons, and the bartender, an elderly man with deep lines etched into his face, nodded sagely. "The manor draws all kinds," he said, his accent rich with the Sussex countryside.

Emily leaned forward. "We're interested in learning more about its history. I'm particularly fascinated by any stories or legends." The bartender exchanged glances with a few patrons, hesitating. Finally, he sighed, pouring two pints of ale. "There's plenty to tell, though not all of it is pleasant."

Over the next hour, patrons tentatively opened about the manor's past. They spoke of the Harlowe family's legacy of wealth marred by tragedy. Generations of Harlowes seemed cursed with misfortune, from mysterious deaths to sudden suicides.

An old man in the pub drew Emily aside and told her that it is rumoured that many generations ago, one of the Harlowes was involved in the British–Egyptian war in 1881 and he had salvaged many valuables from Alexandria just before the British fleet bombarded Alexandria and much of the city was destroyed by fires caused by explosive shells and, according to contemporary British sources. He also told Emily that this gentleman was the first to die under mysterious circumstances.

Rumours persisted of dabbling in dark magic, attempts to cheat death itself. It was said that on certain nights, ghostly figures moved about the manor, the air alive with the whispers of the lost Harlowes. "That place holds onto its dead," an old woman interjected, her voice a whisper above the din. "And those who dare enter often leave... changed."

Returning to the manor, Jeremy and Emily took to exploring its labyrinthine corridors. The dim light from dusty chandeliers cast elongated shadows as they moved from room to room. It was Emily who first found the library—an expansive chamber with shelves that stretched to meet the painted ceiling. "Jeremy, look at this," she called, her voice echoing in the vastness. He joined her, his flashlight beam dancing over the spines of hundreds of books. Many were ancient, their bindings cracked and faded, yet some titles were legible: volumes on history, philosophy, and dark arts. Jeremy's fingers brushed against a tome that slid open easily, revealing a hidden compartment with diaries and letters stacked within.

This reminded Emily of what the old gentleman said in the pub. The valuables that one of the Harlowes brought back from Alexandria may have been ancient documents from the Library of Alexandria, which was famous for housing ancient documents, books, and papyri. "These must have belonged to the Harlowe family," Emily murmured, gingerly picking up a diary. Together, they settled into overstuffed armchairs beneath a dusty chandelier. As lightning flickered outside, they began piecing together the fragmented tale through the writings of Jonathan Harlowe, the manor's last known heir.

In the earliest days of Egyptian history, where pharaohs enacted the will of the gods through the agency of priests, stories of divine quests and the search for immortality filled the sacred halls and writings. Among such seekers of ancient wisdom was Amenemhat, a scholar with a keen interest in early civilisations. His fascination centred on the "Epic of Gilgamesh," revered as one of humanity's oldest narratives. The tale explored themes of heroism, friendship, and a poignant quest for eternal life, embarked upon by the epic's hero, Gilgamesh. For Amenemhat, this saga was more than a mere story; it was a philosophical and esoteric key.

Amenemhat, ignited by initial scholarly admiration, soon found himself consumed by the narrative. The tale of Gilgamesh resonated with him not just as an adventurous story, but as a potential guide to immortality. Of particular intrigue was Enkidu, Gilgamesh's dear companion, whose death catalysed Gilgamesh's journey to Utnapishtim, a human, the sole recipient of divine immortality. Convinced the epic harboured hidden, transformative truths, Amenemhat delved deep into ancient texts, conferring with experts on cuneiform and Mesopotamian religions. He theorised that summoning the spirit of Utnapishtim could unlock secrets to overcoming humanity's mortality, as Utnapishtim had done.

Amenemhat's journals, uncovered by Seti decades later, meticulously recorded his ritualistic endeavours to contact Utnapishtim's spirit. Amenemhat was certain that Utnapishtim's timeless wisdom was the key to immortality. His references to ancient chants and attempts to invoke Utnapishtim through ceremonies merged scholarly practice with the supernatural.

He perceived Utnapishtim as the bearer of knowledge that transcended mortal capabilities. Amenemhat aspired to bridge the gap to divine knowledge through Utnapishtim, seeking to achieve what Gilgamesh could not: eternal life on earth, untouched by divine judgement.

Seti, captivated yet wary, continued Amenemhat's quest. Inspired by his ancestor's writings and a profound fear of mortality, he vowed to succeed where Amenemhat had not. Seti's diary revealed not only scholarly curiosity but also a deep personal desire for lasting permanence, perhaps intensified by witnessing his own lineage's gradual decline.

Seti refined Amenemhat's rituals, blending them with modern interpretations of ancient rites and emerging occult practices. He believed that evoking Utnapishtim required not only historical fidelity but also spiritual resonance, a timeless connection that spanned centuries.

Seti's boldest undertaking strove to metaphorically reverse Utnapishtim's curse—undoing the human doom. He performed these rituals on stormy nights when he felt the boundaries between realms were most tenuous. His accounts describe intricate ceremonies designed to align his soul with ancient wavelengths, seeking to transcend earthly confines.

Jonathan Harlowe first discovered the allure of immortality in his teens, within the shadowy alcoves of his family's extensive library. The Harlowes were a lineage steeped in mystery and academia, each generation leaving behind a legacy of journals and treatises. It was in these writings that Jonathan found frequent references to a name that would capture his imagination.

Jonathan's diary revealed an obsession with extending life—an ambition sparked by his father, Augustus Harlowe, whose relentless pursuit of power and immortality had driven the family to the brink. Augustus had immersed himself in the occult, seeking forbidden knowledge to transcend human limitations. Augustus Harlowe, whose own life was consumed by the quest to transcend mortality. Jonathan noted, in his diary, that Augustus was attracted to Sumerian and Egyptian mythology and occult practices. Emily, through her own study and research, had come across references to the wisdom of Amenemhat.

Augustus had believed that he was Seti reborn and it was his earthly duty to continue the search which Amenemhat and Seti had initiated. The entries spoke of rituals performed in hidden chambers, contracts with shadowy figures, and artefacts imbued with ancient power. The storm raged outside Harlowe Manor, rain lashing against the aged windows like ghosts seeking entrance. In the dimly lit basement, Jonathan Harlowe stood before a mysterious altar, shrouded in the oppressive shadows of history. Flickering candles cast eerie shapes on the stone walls, illuminating the intricate design of sacred geometry that adorned the altar—each angle a testament to the ancient secrets he had so long pursued.

Jonathan believed that what Amenemhat and Seti did not understand was that the power of the ritual was the ritual itself, and he was convinced that the Vedic ritual of Ashvamedha (horse sacrifice) performed by the kings had given them immense power.

Jonathan Harlowe, an erudite scholar deeply fascinated by ancient languages and their mystical applications, had long pondered the efficacy of incantations etched in Sumerian cuneiform. His primary concern was the lack of phonetic authority in these inscriptions. Unlike languages steeped in oral tradition, he speculated that the absence of a consistent phonetic framework might render Sumerian incantations less potent in invoking the desired astral powers. Harlowe theorised that the true power of incantations lay in their oral articulation, where sound and vibration played crucial roles in connecting with higher forces.

This belief led him to explore Sanskrit, especially the rich oral traditions rooted in Vedic practices. Sanskrit, as spoken and chanted by Vedic Brahmin priests in ancient kings' courts, dating back to around 4000 BC, was revered for its purported ability to channel cosmic energies through its precise phonetic delivery. To delve deeper into this tradition, Jonathan embarked on a journey to India, where he immersed himself in the serene environment of an ashram. There, he dedicated himself to studying Sanskrit under the guidance of knowledgeable scholars and practising priests. His experience within the ashram exposed him to the rhythmic chanting and the detailed rituals that illustrated the profound impact tonal quality had on incantations.

Through this rigorous study and practice, Harlowe came to appreciate the nuanced power of Sanskrit in spiritual ceremonies. He observed how its carefully crafted syllables and cadence seemed to harness and direct spiritual energies more effectively than the static and silent cuneiform symbols could. This eye-opening journey shifted his perspective, solidifying his belief in the unparalleled potency of oral traditions, particularly those of the Vedic Sanskrit lineage.

Tonight marked the culmination of his obsession: to transcend the boundary between life and death. Clutching a weathered tome filled with Vedic incantations, Jonathan placed a pure white horse from his stable, tranquil yet ominous, upon the altar. The animal seemed oddly calm amid the chaos of the storm, its eyes reflecting the flickering candlelight with an otherworldly depth.

Thunder crashed as Jonathan began to chant the sacred incantation. The words rolled off his tongue, carrying the weight of centuries, rising amidst the cacophony of the storm. The air crackled with energy, charged with anticipation. As he spoke, shadows around him morphed into figures lost to time, whispering half-formed memories that echoed through the damp air.

Suddenly, a violent shudder rattled the manor, and the altar vibrated with intensity. A luminous sphere erupted above it, casting blinding light that pierced the darkness. Jonathan felt a magnetic pull, the veil between the realms thinning dangerously, the line between life and death blurring.

Yet, with such power came a burden. The spirit of the horse, now aglow with divine energy, consumed the physical manifestation and shimmered before him in a radiant form. "What you seek is powerful, but desire carries a price," it intoned, its voice resonating through the basement like rolling thunder.

In that moment, Jonathan understood. Sacrifice was not merely the offering of flesh; it was the relinquishing of the past, the essence of his sorrow and love. With a heavy heart, he surrendered these memories to the storm, igniting the sphere in a brilliant flash.

As the light consumed the basement, the echoes of Jonathan Harlowe's choice intertwined with the storm's fury. The old manor would never be the same, forever haunted by the whispers of life and death that danced in the shadows, a testament to his desperate leap into the unknown.

Both Augustus and Jonathan were consumed by their pursuits. Their diaries, filled with cryptic lines and fervent appeals to Amenemhat, left a legacy shrouded in both intrigue and tragedy. The manor stood as a silent witness to their endeavours, charged with the energies and echoes of their relentless quest.

This ambition, while never wholly realised, bound their souls to the manor, their efforts echoing through the generations. It was this very pursuit that set the stage for the spectral horrors and mysteries that Jeremy and Emily would soon uncover as they probed deeper into Harlowe Manor's secrets—secrets that spoke of the eternal human longing to wrest control from the hands of fate and forge a path into the forever unknown. But their pursuit came at a cost. The lines between life and death were blurred, and the manor became a vessel for restless spirits.

Jonathan described terrifying visions and sleepless nights filled with spectral visitations. The family's tragedies, once thought to be mere misfortune, were revealed as retributions from forces beyond their understanding, forces provoked by the elder Harlowe's hubris. Emily was particularly taken by an entry detailing a failed rite of transmigration on a stormy night—an attempt to transfer souls into new vessels that resulted in unspeakable horrors.

"Jonathan tried to achieve immortality by transferring his soul," Emily noted, her voice laced with academic excitement. "It's like karma functioned as a check, amplifying the consequences of their actions and binding them to the manor." Emily's fascination with soul transmigration was rooted in her belief that the soul carried imprints of its past interactions, creating a cycle of influence spanning multiple lifetimes. Her research proposed that intense emotions and unresolved debts could trap souls in certain places, perpetuating a cycle of suffering.

"Jonathan's notes mention the karmic backlash," she explained to Jeremy. "Their actions left unresolved energies in this world, effectively anchoring their souls to the manor." Jeremy nodded, absorbing the gravity of their findings. "And if these energies are stirred, perhaps by new residents like us…" he let the thought hang in the air, the implications clear. Together, they speculated that understanding the Harlowes' rituals might reveal.

It began with the cold spots—sudden, inexplicable chills that seemed to emanate from nowhere, brushing against the skin like icy fingers. Jeremy first noticed them during a brisk walk through the drawing room, the temperature dropping sharply, causing his breath to form misty clouds. Emily joined him, her analytical mind struggling to rationalise the invisible force fields that seemed to drift through the corridors.

The whispers came next—soft, indistinct murmurs that hung just out of earshot, like echoes of conversations held long ago. One evening, as Emily reviewed the Harlowes' diaries in the dim light of her study lamp, she heard them—a faint chorus of voices, weaving through the silence. When she looked up, she was alone. Yet, the sense of being observed remained a constant, unsettling presence.

Shadowy figures, too, began to make their appearances. At first, they were glitches in the periphery of vision, dismissed as tricks of the fading light. But as days passed, Jeremy and Emily could no longer deny their presence. These phantoms flitted near doorways, lingered in empty rooms, and seemed particularly drawn to the manor's library, where Jonathan and Augustus Harlowe had chronicled their pursuits. One night, as a storm raged outside, Jeremy ventured down to the grand hall, where he encountered a silhouette by the hearth. Startled, he called out, but the figure dissipated into the air, leaving only the scent of damp earth in its wake.

Both Jeremy and Emily began experiencing vivid dreams, as if the manor's lingering soul had seeped into their subconscious. Jeremy found himself in 19th-century attire, standing in the manor's ballroom. The room was filled with elegantly dressed spectres, their laughter echoing eerily. He danced with a woman he had never met, her features obscured, yet hauntingly familiar. As the dream progressed, faces warped, revealing ghastly expressions of despair.

Emily's dreams took a darker turn. She often relived the final days of Jonathan Harlowe—immersed in his desperation, feeling the weight of his futile rituals. One particularly vivid dream placed her in the midst of a stormy night, as Jonathan frantically recited invocations, the air around him shimmering with a strange luminescence. She could feel his fear and determination, his chilling awareness of the abyss he had opened. The line between their waking and dream worlds began to blur, causing unified hesitation between them. Tension flared, eroding the camaraderie that had initially bonded them.

"Are you sure you're not just... seeing what you want to see?" Jeremy challenged Emily one evening, his scepticism a defence against the mounting dread. They sat surrounded by candlelight, wary even of their own shadows.

"I've been sceptical too, Jeremy," Emily replied, her eyes wide with insistence. "But these dreams, these experiences—they can't be mere coincidences. We've become part of the manor's story." Their arguments often revolved around their interpretations of supernatural events. Jeremy clung to facts, wary of the very wonders that had initially drawn him to journalism, while Emily urged a more open-minded exploration of the manor's uncanny happenings.

As days melded into one another, their investigations took a toll. Both grappled with insomnia, their minds racing with questions. The manor seemed to amplify their fears, mirroring the Harlowes' tragic descent into obsession and isolation. Emily's belief in spiritual resonance clashed with Jeremy's demand for tangible proof. Yet, despite their differences, a shared resolve drove them to uncover the truth haunting Harlowe.

Back in the manor's library, Jeremy and Emily pored over the Harlowe diaries and tomes unearthed from their exploration. The prospect of liberating trapped souls was daunting, but within the cryptic writings, they found clues—a potential path to redemption for both the manor and themselves.

Emily, drawing from her research into consciousness and the occult, suggested they perform a cleansing ritual—a synthesis of the Harlowes' own practices with elements meant to bring peace rather than power. The goal was simple yet profound: to close the painful loop of karma that chained the family's spirits to their earthly bindings.

The diary entry that Jeremy and Emily discovered in the depths of Harlowe Manor revealed more than the rituals and obsessions of Jonathan Harlowe. It contained a vivid, unsettling vision in which Jonathan, experiencing a deep regression into his karmic past, found himself transported to the time of the Spanish Inquisition.

In the dim whisper of candlelight that flickered across the library walls, Jonathan described his vision with harrowing clarity. It occurred during one of his most desperate attempts to grasp the nature of his soul's entanglements. Surrounded by the symbols and implements of his ritual, Jonathan felt an overwhelming force pulling him backward through the corridors of time, beyond the confines of Harlowe Manor, into a dark era defined by fear and unyielding authority— the Spanish Inquisition.

In this vision, he was not Jonathan Harlowe, an Englishman seeking immortality, but an executioner—a man tasked with the grim duty of enforcing religious orthodoxy through brutal means. He wore the heavy robes of his station, the hood casting shadows over his visage, hiding his identity from those who stood pleading in chains before the tribunal. The aura of authority clung to him like a second skin, yet beneath it simmered a brewing storm of doubt and remorse.

As he stood in the cold stone chamber of the inquisition, Jonathan perceived the faces of the accused—men, women, and sometimes children—whose only crime was divergence in belief or practice, perceived heresies in the rigid theology of the time. Their eyes, wide with fear yet flickering with defiance, pierced through the thin veil of his official duties and into the depths of his hidden conscience.

Jonathan's detailed account captured moments where the clang of chains echoed like mournful chimes, resonating within him as a counterpoint to the relentless chants of the faithful, calling for purity at any cost. His soul recoiled at every edict passed, every pyre lit, each soul condemned not only by the dictates of the inquisitors but by his own hand—a chilling reminder of the power he wielded and the injustice with which he wielded it.

The vision revealed the core of his existential torment: in the pursuit of duty and a twisted sense of righteousness, he had extinguished life and love without reflection on the far-reaching consequences. As the flames rose, illuminating the faces of those he condemned, Jonathan felt their cries as physical pain—a searing ache that transcended his temporal self and reverberated through the scenario of his spiritual existence.

Herein lay the karmic roots of his later obsession with defeating death, a subliminal desire to atone for the souls he helped dispatch into the void, seeking a form of penance through the mastery of mortality. It was a ghostly cycle he sought to break, yet never fully understood; in trying to defy the natural order, he mirrored his inquisitional self, imposing his will upon the fabric of life with relentless fervour.

As Jonathan's vision faded, and he was thrust back into the reality of his library with heart pounding and skin chilled, he realised the magnitude of his karmic legacy. He scribbled desperately in his diary, a plea not just for understanding but for release from the repeating patterns of darkness that shadowed his incarnations.

Jonathan's entry provided Jeremy and Emily with invaluable insight into the depth of the Harlowes' spiritual legacy—a potent reminder that the cycles of oppression and suffering often perpetuate until consciously recognised and intentionally interrupted. Through his vision, they saw the same conflicts mirrored across time, humanity's perpetual struggle between the pursuit of power and the necessity of redemption.

Understanding this karmic entanglement allowed them to approach their ritual with deeper empathy and resolve, the weight of history urging them toward not just liberation for the Harlowes, but for all souls bound by the unseen chains of time—urging them to confront, integrate, and ultimately transform the shadows that linger across generations.

"Their rituals didn't fail because they were inherently flawed," Emily explained. "They failed because they were fuelled by selfish intent. Ours must be different, focused on release and forgiveness."

The basement of Harlow Manor was a shrine of half-fulfilled intentions and restless spirits. Flickering candles cast eerie shadows on the damp stone walls, their warmth barely making a dent in the chilling atmosphere. Emily and Jeremy, believing they can free the Harlowe spirits from their earthly shackles, entered the basement. But unbeknownst to them, the manor harboured a darker, more profound secret—a thread of karmic negativity that wove itself through the very core of the ritual, binding them in an inescapable web.

In the days following their apparent triumph, a troubling connection began to manifest between the two. Each night, as twilight wrapped the manor in its nocturnal embrace, they were haunted by vivid dreams—visions of the Harlowes, their sorrowful faces pleading for finality, for something left undone. Their cries became an unholy symphony, resonating in the quiet corners of Emily and Jeremy's minds. What they thought was liberation was merely the beginning of their descent.

Compelled by an unease he could not shake, Jeremy ventured back to the ruins alone one evening, sensing an insidious pull that beckoned him back to the site of their ritual. He stood where the grand library once flourished, now a mere shadow of its former self. The air crackled with an unnatural energy as if the manor were aware of his presence, watching, waiting. As the moon hid behind a blanket of clouds, a chill pervaded the atmosphere, thickening to a suffocating density.

Without warning, the earth quaked beneath him, the stones of the manor shifting and rearranging as if possessed by a violent force. They formed a narrowing circle around him, a prison crafted by the very essence of his unaddressed sins. Caught in this sinister embrace, Jeremy felt the remnants of the ritual's power encircle him. The cemetery of spirits he thought he had liberated was reawakening, awakening not as protectors but as harbingers of a more profound truth—a truth steeped in the consequences of their unfinished personal burdens.

Meanwhile, Emily, consumed by an inexplicable sense of urgency, followed her instincts to find him. The energy of their bond drove her deeper into the ruins, leading her into the heart of the trap unknowingly set. Upon arriving, she found Jeremy encircled, his stark expression painted with the strokes of fear and realization—two souls entwined not in freedom, but in the inescapable web of their own unresolved ethics.

Desperation clawed at her heart, and without a moment's hesitation, she crossed the threshold of the cold circle, sacrificing her own liberty to join him. In that instant, their fates became irreversibly intertwined, caught in the manor's final, tragic grasp. Together, they realized that the ritual they performed had not resolved their inner turmoil but merely transferred the weight of their karmic baggage onto the very fabric of Harlow Manor itself.

The spirits they had thought liberated were not gone; rather, they had become the essence of the unresolved grief and anxiety that now bound Emily and Jeremy. Their guilt, their unaddressed sorrow, had transformed into the manor's anchors—demanding acknowledgment in a final act of desperation for clarity. Beneath the walls of Harlow Manor, thunder rumbled ominously above, and lightning pierced through the heavens, illuminating the scene—a cataclysmic prelude to their doom.

As the storm intensified, the walls of the basement began to close in. The manor, sensing its impending collapse, tightened its grip on the two souls it had chosen to reclaim. The echoes of the spirits mingled with the sound of thunder, swirling into a cacophony that reverberated through the chamber. Emily and Jeremy, instead of being freed, were consumed by the very energies they had sought to cleanse. Their desires for redemption and liberation proved futile against the heavy weight of their karmic negativity.

In a final cataclysmic unfolding, the basement of Harlow Manor began to cave in. The walls shuddered, and the roof cracked, as if the very foundation of the place was mourning their tragic fate. In that moment, the realization crushed down upon them that true cleansing demanded not just an act of will but a deep surrender to the past—an acceptance of the mistakes and pains that had shaped their lives.

As the sun rose the next morning, Harlow Manor stood in ruin—a broken monument to incomplete journeys. The spirits of the Harlowes, now intertwined with Emily and Jeremy, melded into the very essence of the land that was once theirs. The realm of the living and the dead converged in a spiral of liberation and loss, leaving behind only whispers carried by the winds. Their physical forms faded into the myths that would be told in hushed tones, a cautionary tale about the complexities of atonement and the unbreakable threads of karmic ties.

Emily and Jeremy had sought to perform a cleansing ritual, yet they could not escape the tendencies that held them fast. They had entered Harlow Manor in search of redemption, wishing to free the spirits of the Harlowe family from their torment, but in doing so, they overlooked the truths that resided within themselves. The power of the ritual they performed was not merely an act of purification; it was a profound mirror reflecting their unresolved traumas and karmic debts—bonds they had yet to confront.

As the walls of the basement finally crumbled, sealing their fate in the rubble of Harlow Manor, the grandeur of the estate bore witness to the chaos generated by their desperate attempts at liberation. Thunder echoed through the night, the wind howled like a chorus of spirits long forgotten, and the manor itself trembled as if lamenting the loss of its last two inhabitants, a final admonition against the dangers of superficial attempts at cleansing.

The story of the Harlowe spirits, entwined now with Emily and Jeremy's souls, would echo through generations, a haunting reminder that true freedom requires more than good intentions; it demands the courageous confrontation of one's personal darkness. Those who would dare approach the ruins henceforth would hear the winds carrying whispers— tales of bravery turned to folly, where the unaddressed past intertwined tragically with the present.

In the months that followed, nature began to reclaim Harlow Manor. Vines wrapped around the cracked stones, flowers grew in vibrant defiance of the despair that once filled its halls, and an air of melancholic beauty enveloped the ruins. Birds nested in the remnants of the rafters, and the rustle of the wind played a soft melody through the broken windows, a serene juxtaposition to the chaos that had transpired within. Locals spoke of the area reverently, sharing stories of a place heavy with energy—a sanctuary of sorts, forever marked by the presence of those who had bound their destinies to the manor.

In this rebirth of nature, the lesson of Emily and Jeremy transcended mere myth. The whispers of their sacrifice became a rallying cry for those seeking true inner peace, urging future generations to delve deeply into self-reflection before attempting to rid themselves of entanglements. The Harlowe story became emblematic of the eternal struggle between light and darkness, knowledge and ignorance—a reminder of the necessity for healing from within before seeking to uplift others.

People from neighbouring towns came to ponder the ruins, driven by curiosity and spiritual inquiry. Some sought solace, while others tried to connect with the realm of the spirits, warning each other of the dangers embedded in hasty rituals. The collective fear and respect that grew around the remnants of Harlow Manor transformed the site into a place of pilgrimage, drawing those who understood the weight of unresolved burdens.

And yet, there were still some who attempted to conduct their rituals under the guise of cleansing, oblivious to the lesson steeped in the manor's tragic tale. They fell victim to the same traps, blindly stepping into the cold circles of energy that awaited them within the ruins. One by one, they too found themselves ensnared in the gravitational pull of their own unaddressed karma, the spirits of the Harlowes now awakened as allies of judgment.

The cycle perpetuated itself, echoing through time, a concert of betrayal and redemption. With each new attempt at purification mingled with unresolved issues, the manor would claim another pair of souls, gradually building a sanctuary where the remnants of despair were interwoven with the quest for understanding. The restless spirits danced among the ruins, each new arrival joining their hallowed ranks, forever bound by the shared lessons of struggle, the futility of superficial cleansing, and the eternal quest for true liberation.

As years turned into decades, the tale of Harlow Manor became enshrined in folklore, a story passed from elder to child, imbued with a sense of caution and reverence. It served as an enduring metaphor for the human experience—of facing one's shadows, recognizing the depths of personal history, and the importance of connection in healing.

In the end, Harlow Manor stood as a testament to both the futility and necessity of confronting our darkest selves. Emily and Jeremy's story transformed into a vital lesson embedded in the fabric of the community—a reminder that the capacity for liberation resides within each individual, patiently awaiting acknowledgment and reconciliation with the past. The manor, even in ruin, became a beacon, guiding souls toward a notion of redemption that was holistic, compassionate, and unforgiving in its demand for authenticity.

And so, as whispers of the Harlowe spirits flowed gently through the trees, the cycle of liberation and loss continued to spin its intricate web—inviting all who ventured near to contemplate the delicate balance of intent, action, and the intricate scenario of human experience, forever intertwining their lives with those who have come before.

WEB OF TANGLED REALITY

Dr Alistair Grant, a well-regarded anaesthesiologist at King's College London, was known not only for his medical expertise but also for pursuing the mysteries of human consciousness. His fascination lay particularly with the phenomena of near-death and out-of-body experiences, realms that merged the scientific with the mystical. His office, nestled within the venerable walls of the college, served as a sanctuary for his research. The space was a scholarly labyrinth of journals, papers, and texts, each page dedicated to unravelling the enigma of human awareness. It was a place that thrummed with the intellectual vigour of London's academic heart, where ideas flowed as freely as the Thames nearby.

In this office, Alistair immersed himself in studying the intricate dance between the anaesthetised mind and the boundaries of life and death. His work was an exploration not just of medical science but also of the philosophical questions that tug at the edges of human understanding. Earlier that evening, Alistair had delivered a captivating lecture on altered states of consciousness. Alistair, deeply immersed in his exploration of human consciousness, found himself captivated by the transition state between waking and dreaming. This liminal space, rich with potential, echoed the tales of the Vedic Puranas, particularly the enigmatic experiences of King Janaka.

Janaka's journeys in consciousness, where reality and dream intertwined, became a foundation for Alistair's understanding of panpsychism, the belief that consciousness is a universal feature of all things. Inspired, Alistair crafted a narrative where his protagonist, an interstellar traveler, harnesses this transitional state to navigate alternate realms, discovering ancient truths and bridging distant worlds through the veiled corridors of the mind. His students were enraptured, hanging onto his every word as he spoke of consciousness as a fluid spectrum that could reach beyond ordinary limits. He suggested that such a spectrum allowed glimpses into a profound interconnectedness binding all existence. Alistair's lectures weren't merely academic—they were a call to explore the depths of human experience. His voice echoed with the conviction of a man who had peered into the depths and returned with tales from the brink.

As the evening waned, and the afterglow of intellectual exchange dimmed into quietude, Alistair found himself back in his office. The room's warm, familiar ambience began to weave a cocoon around him, and sitting in his worn leather chair, he felt the gentle tug of fatigue. The steady ticking of the clock and the soft rustle of papers seemed to harmonise with the distant hum of the city night, creating a lullaby that coaxed his eyelids to droop.

Slowly, the boundary between reality and dreams began to blur. Alistair's head nodded forward, and he slipped into a dream-filled slumber. Here, in this ephemeral abode, his mind was liberated from the constraints of waking reality. His thoughts floated freely, melding realities, and suspending the rigidity of time. In this altered state, Alistair was no longer bound to the corporeal constraints of his office or the academic rigour of his inquiries. Instead, he was whisked away into the boundless landscape of dreams where worlds interconnected, realms converged, and the mysteries of consciousness awaited his exploration.

As he sank deeper into this dream world, potential insights danced before him like flickering shadows, suggesting answers to the very questions he pursued so ardently in the waking hours. The night's embrace promised a journey into places where the waking mind dared to tread lightly, but where the dreaming mind ventured boldly. Some might call it escapism, but for Dr Alistair Grant, this was a voyage—a traversal of the bridges he sought to build in his ceaseless quest to understand the fabric of consciousness.

In the dreamscape where Alistair found himself as King Amara, the world was a scenario of vibrant colours and harmonious sounds. The sky stretched in endless azure, kissed by sunlight that danced upon the verdant earth below. Here in this lush realm, the air was perpetually infused with the sweet fragrance of exotic flowers, their hues so vivid they appeared almost otherworldly. Birdsong harmonised with the gentle rustling of leaves, creating a symphony that celebrated life in its purest form.

Amid this idyllic setting lived Amelie, whose wisdom and presence were as profound as the mountains that cradled their village. She was the community's spiritual guide, her eyes a deep well of understanding and compassion. Each gesture, rich with grace, spoke a language older than words — a language that resonated deeply with Alistair.

Their relationship blossomed naturally, beginning with moments shared during tribal ceremonies where Alistair observed Amelie invoking the spirits of ancestors. She would move with a fluid precision, her voice interlacing with the chants of the villagers, creating a palpable connection between the present and the realms beyond. Alistair was captivated by these rituals, finding in them a profound echo of the consciousness studies he had pursued in his waking life.

Under Amelie's guidance, Alistair delved into the tribe's spiritual practices. He learned of the sacred groves where they honoured the cycles of life and death, of the river rituals symbolising renewal and continuity. Each tradition wove a deeper understanding and respect for the interconnectedness of all beings. Alistair was particularly intrigued by the ancestor dance — a ceremonial gathering where stories of the past were spun into vibrant reenactments, celebrating the wisdom of their forebears and weaving it into the fabric of current existence.

As the seasons unfolded, Alistair and Amelie's connection deepened, blossoming into a love that mirrored the vibrant world around them. She taught him to listen to the whispers of the earth, to understand the subtle signs present in every natural occurrence. Their days were filled with laughter and discovery, exploring sacred spaces, and sharing silent reveries at sunset.

When Alistair asked Amelie to be his wife, it was during the harvest festival, a time marked by joy and abundance. The tribe gathered to celebrate their union, a vivid tableau of colour and song. Alistair marvelled at the intricacy of the ceremonial garments, adorned with symbols of prosperity and unity. The celebration was not just of love, but of community, linking each individual to the cosmos.

Life with Amelie brought Alistair a profound joy he had never imagined. They were soon blessed with a son, a curious child with eyes that mirrored his mother's wisdom and his father's wonder. Their home was a haven filled with laughter, shared stories, and the constant rhythm of nature. Parenthood, for Alistair, became a daily lesson in humility and awe, deepening his understanding of consciousness as a continuum extending beyond physical life.

The vibrant scenario of their existence was punctuated by simple, joyful moments — teaching their son to swim in the sparkling river, sharing meals with their extended family under a sky ablaze with stars. These experiences brought a deep fulfilment that resonated within Alistair's heart, solidifying his identity not as the aloof academic of his past but as a beloved leader, a devoted husband, and an adoring father in this dream world that had become irresistibly real.

Alistair woke up slowly, the familiar confines of his library coming into focus through a haze of confusion. The room was dimly lit, the evening sun casting long shadows across his cluttered desk. He blinked, attempting to shake off the vivid remnants of his dream. Yet, the echoes of that other world—the vibrant colours, the harmonious sounds, the warmth of Amelie's hand—clung to him like a heavy mist, refusing to dissipate.

The dream had not been like any other ephemeral night vision; it had enveloped him in a sensual scenario of emotions and sensations so poignant that reality seemed pale in comparison. Alistair sat motionless, the realisation settling over him like a shroud: he was alone. The connection to Amelie, the laughter of their son, the sense of belonging in that other life—all were illusions woven deep within his subconscious.

The pang of loss was unexpected and acute. It gnawed at the edges of his contentment, as insistent as the ticking clock on the mantelpiece that marked the passage of moments in this otherwise silent room. Alistair found himself grasping at the fading threads of the dream, desperately attempting to retain the warmth and clarity of those cherished experiences, but they slipped through his fingers like grains of sand.

His thoughts were a turbulent sea of conflicting emotions. In the world of the waking, Alistair was a respected anaesthesiologist, celebrated for his academic contributions and revered by his students for his insights into consciousness. His career had been built meticulously, brick by brick, on hours of research and dedication. Yet now, these accomplishments felt hollow, overshadowed by the depth of life experienced within the dream.

The steady rhythms of his daily existence—a series of lectures, discussions with colleagues, and tireless evenings spent poring over journals—suddenly seemed devoid of the vibrancy that had defined them. Each familiar face, each movement through his life's routines, was underscored by absence. The absence of Amelie's touch, the absence of his son's laughter, the absence of a life filled with joy and profound spiritual connection.

This internal disquiet began to erode his satisfaction, a relentless tide wearing down his once-stalwart resolve. Alistair questioned the reality he inhabited: Was this the life he was meant to live, or merely a shadow cast by the dreams his soul longed to inhabit? As weeks passed, colleagues noted a change in him—his conversations took on an existential edge, laced with uncharacteristic melancholy.

Alistair became introspective, ensnared by the complexities of his longing. The dissonance between his two existences consumed his waking hours. Nights were spent staring into the darkness, seeking answers that lay beyond the grasp of conscious reasoning. His heart ached with an unspoken yearning, a desire imbued with the pain of knowing what was possible, only to have it cruelly snatched away.

This internal conflict birthed a profound sense of alienation. Alistair felt untethered from his achievements, distanced from the identity he had constructed. He wandered through his life as an outsider, a man caught between two worlds—one where he was fulfilled, another where fulfilment eluded him with every passing day.

The days following Alistair's searing dream of Amelie and their son were suffused with an insistent, unshakable question: What if the dream was not a mere figment of his subconscious but a glimpse into another existence—a parallel universe where his heart's desires were lived and breathed into reality? This intrusive thought dug deep into his mind, planting seeds of doubt and yearning that sprouted into a consuming obsession.

Alistair found himself ensconced in his office, surrounded by towering stacks of books and articles. His once orderly system of notetaking devolved into a chaotic array of scribbled thoughts scattered across pages—a visual representation of the tumult within. He plunged into texts on consciousness, quantum theory, parallel worlds, and ancient philosophies, desperate for a thread of evidence to anchor his spiralling thoughts.

His quest for understanding was relentless and all-consuming. Alistair's nights were spent poring over writings that suggested consciousness might transcend the physical realm, that dreams could be windows into alternate realities. These possibilities, once considered speculative at best, now seemed like the only plausible answer to the profound experiences of his dreamworld.

As his academic obsession grew, so did his isolation. He withdrew from social engagements, ignoring messages from friends and neglecting familial connections. Conversations that once flowed with ease felt burdensome; each encounter a reminder of his dissatisfaction with his life. The vibrant community he believed he had found with Amelie and their son seemed so real, making his actual existence feel unbearably dull by comparison.

Professional relationships began to fray as Alistair's distraction became evident. Colleagues who were once confidantes noticed the shift—the faraway look in his eyes during meetings, the forgetfulness during discussions, the uncharacteristic absenteeism from gatherings he'd once led. His mind constantly drifted, wandering through labyrinths of thought and theory, searching for a way to reconcile his experiences.

In the lecture hall, where Alistair had always held sway with his captivating insights into human consciousness, a noticeable shift occurred. His lectures, formerly structured and enlightening, transformed into rambling discourses dominated by existential musings and speculative theories. Students who had thrived under his tutelage began to whisper concerns about his well-being, their notes filled with fragmented ideas and overarching questions rather than structured knowledge.

Alistair's persistent focus on questions of reality and existence eclipsed practical teaching. He would stand before the class, oftentimes silent, consumed by thoughts, before launching into soliloquies on the nature of being and non-being, blurring the lines between lecture and philosophical ponderings. His fervour for his subject, while earnest, took on a morose edge, one that hinted at a man adrift without anchor.

Despite attempts by a few close colleagues to reach out, Alistair remained guarded, his soul fixated on a truth only he could perceive. Invitations to discuss upcoming research collaborations were declined; casual conversations were truncated as he retreated deeper into his private world. He became a shadow in the halls, present yet absent, his focus narrowed perilously to this singular obsession.

In this relentless pursuit of understanding, Alistair's world contracted sharply, reducing the once expansive richness of his reality to a solitary quest for answers. Every interaction, every divergence from his research felt like an intrusion, an intolerable distraction from discovering the truth he so desperately sought—a truth that lay tantalisingly beyond the veil of his dreaming mind.

Though his body was back in the waking world, remnants of his dream life lingered painfully. The memory of his wife, his child, and the life they shared pressed down on him like a heavy mantle he could never cast off. The son he had loved did not exist in his real life—his waking life where he remained childless, bound by the steady ticking of the clock and the weight of his endless quest for understanding.

This vivid, alternate existence ignited a lifelong obsession in Alistair: the desire to discern what constituted reality. Was the life he awoke to more genuine than the one he had dreamed? The questions became an insatiable longing to bridge the divide between the realms, to reclaim the son he felt slipping into the depths of his subconscious.

In the days that followed, Alistair immersed himself even deeper into his studies, scouring texts and engaging with colleagues in philosophical dialogues. He explored theories of consciousness that suggested all experiences, dreamt or lived, were facets of a greater reality intertwined with the fabric of existence. His profound journey left an indelible mark, inspiring others through his lectures and writings on the nature of consciousness, reality, and the interconnectedness of all life.

Alistair's days were now punctuated by a fervent exploration into the esoteric and spiritual realms, a path that promised answers beyond the empirical boundaries of his scientific discipline. Books on astral projection, ancient mysticism, and sacred rituals cluttered his already cramped study, each a beacon of potential insights into transcending ordinary consciousness. These texts, rich with tales of mystics who claimed to walk between worlds, captivated him, suggesting that his cherished dream life was not only possible but perhaps accessible through intentioned effort.

By night, Alistair submerged himself in meditation, viewing it as a bridge between the waking world and the vibrant land where Amelie and his son lived. He practised diligently, experimenting with techniques drawn from various traditions—Tibetan dream yoga, shamanic journeying, and Sufi whirling—all aimed at expanding his awareness and slipping the bonds of his physical form. He spent hours in lotus position, eyes closed, breathing measured and deep as he envisioned the lush landscapes and the warmth of his family's embrace. Initially, meditation brought peace and moments of clarity, illuminating brief flashes of the dream realm. Yet as his dedication grew fervent, demanding longer sessions and deeper focus, it strained his mental and spiritual limits. Extended meditation veered into sleepless nights, and the boundary between meditation and dreaming blurred, each foray a quest to spill into that other reality. His grip on mere consciousness loosened, leaving him susceptible to hallucinations that both tantalised and tormented him—Amelie's laughter in the rustle of wind, his son's small hand tugging at his own.

In pursuit of altered states, Alistair began incorporating herbal infusions known for their psychoactive properties. Mushrooms and roots, traditionally deemed sacred among shamans, found their way into his regimen, each dose a step further into the unknown. These attempts often left him in narcotic trances, caught between worlds but never fully crossed over. Consequently, his health began to wane. Once robust, his frame thinned, cheekbones casting sharp shadows under the harsh light of his study. His skin took on a pallor that belied the feverish intensity that fuelled his days and nights.

Colleagues grew increasingly concerned, noting the dark circles under his eyes and his absent gestures, their attempts at intervention meeting a man both intensely focused and strangely detached. Alistair's formal demeanour cracked, revealing a man who seemed exhausted not only by his pursuits but by the weight of dual realities.

Mentally, he grappled with questions that had no easy answers—were these pursuits revealing a new path of understanding or pushing him to the brink of madness? The dream family he longed for felt achingly real, yet with every attempted journey, they remained unconquerably out of reach. He oscillated between hope and despair, an emotional pendulum swinging wildly with each session that brought him closer yet maintained the insurmountable chasm.

Alistair's endeavour to reconnect with his dream life, a journey founded on the promise of reunion and transcendent truth, threatened to unravel his very being. In the quiet depths of another slumber,

Alistair once again found himself slipping effortlessly into the dreamscape that had come to feel like home. He was pulled back into the realm where he had lived as King Amara, eager to rejoin Amelie and their son in the harmony and fulfilment that their world promised. But unlike the vibrant, harmonious world he remembered, this visit was different from the start.

The world that materialised around him was shrouded in a sombre twilight, the once vibrant colours now muted and washed out. The sky hung heavy above a landscape that seemed alien despite its familiar contours. As Alistair searched for his wife and child, he felt a chill, creeping sense of despair threading its way through everything around him.

It wasn't long before he found them. Amelie stood before him, but she was altered—her radiant beauty dulled, her skin pale, her eyes filled with an anguish that struck him to his core. Their son stood by her side: thin, gaunt, and frail, with none of the boundless curiosity and vitality that Alistair cherished. They were ravaged by hunger and lived under the shadow of poverty, starkly contrasting with the abundant life he remembered.

Alistair's heart sank as he struggled to comprehend what had happened. How could this world, once so overflowing with life and joy, have deteriorated so drastically? Despite his role as King Amara, he found himself helpless in the face of their suffering and unable to alleviate their plight. The despair in Amelie's eyes was a mirror of his own, reflecting a shared sense of loss and fear that had no remedy in either dream or reality.

The urgency of their situation demanded action, prompting them to leave the kingdom of Amara in search of a better life. This new journey was fraught with danger and uncertainty. They set out through a dense forest, its once familiar paths now twisted and obscured by shadows. The trees loomed above, their branches tangled and woven into a near-impenetrable canopy. As they ventured deeper, Alistair felt the weight of the forest's oppressive presence, as if it were a living entity intent on assessing their resolve.

In this labyrinthine wilderness, Alistair experienced strange episodes of disorientation. He could only catch intermittent glimpses of Amelie and his son through the underbrush. Each brief sighting filled him with both relief and anxiety. Were they truly just ahead, or were they spectres conjured by his own desperate yearning?

As the daylight faded, the forest began to reveal its mysteries—strange and ominous creatures emerged from the shadows, curious yet menacing. These visitors took on myriad forms, as if plucked from the depths of mythology and nightmare: ghostly figures flitting between trees, eyes gleaming with unknowable intentions, and creatures with shifting shapes that defied logic, evoking awe and dread.

The oppressive atmosphere weighed heavily on Alistair's spirit. Somehow, he sensed that these creatures were manifestations not just of the forest, but of his own fear and despair—psychic echoes of his helplessness and guilt about Amelie's altered state and their son's distress. The forest seemed alive with whispered voices that gnawed at his resolve, infusing his sense of purpose with doubt and confusion.

The moments of clarity, when he could briefly see his family again, served as beacons of hope amid the gloom. Yet each sighting was fleeting, leaving him more disoriented than before. Alistair called out to them, but his voice seemed swallowed by the dense forest air. Brief responses floated back to him: the distant sound of Amelie's comforting voice or their son's faint laughter, both laced with an undercurrent of urgency that spurred him forward despite the growing darkness.

The climax of their journey came when Alistair, in his frantic search, was confronted by the most fearsome apparition yet: a massive werewolf—a creature of legend and terror, born of the shadows and the very heart of his deepest fears. Its eyes glowed an eerie red in the forest's twilight, staring straight into Alistair's soul, challenging him to confront his inner turmoil.

Paralysed by a mixture of fear and fascination, Alistair felt as if time froze in that moment. The werewolf opened its gaping jaws, revealing sharp teeth glistening like daggers in the fading light. Alistair was helpless to resist as the beast lunged toward him, jaws closing around him, the darkness consuming all.

With a violent jolt, Alistair awoke in his library, heart pounding as if to burst, the echo of the werewolf's growl still reverberating in his ears. His body was drenched with sweat, the room's once-comfortable warmth now stifling. The realisation that he was safe within his real-world sanctuary offered little comfort against the haunting vividness of the dream.

As he struggled to calm his racing heart, Alistair couldn't shake the lingering dread and profound sense of his helplessness. As he dived deeper into the realm linking dreams and wakefulness, the multiplicity of his existence both expanded and fractured, the collision of realities mounting an unspeakable complexity that eroded the solid grounding of his former self.

Alistair's journey towards transcendence began as a whisper, a quiet insinuation that grew louder with each passing day, beseeching him to consider the unthinkable: abandoning the waking world entirely. This notion, initially quelled by his ties to reason and rationality, slowly emerged as a compelling solution to his existential longing. His academic career, friendships, and worldly possessions became shadows, mere ornaments of a reality that seemed increasingly irrelevant compared to the visceral truth of his dream life.

The decision crystallised one evening as he sat alone in his study, the moonlight casting silver streaks through the window. It was a moment of acute clarity, born not out of despair but profound resolve. Alistair realised that his vision was not meant to be fleeting; it was an invitation to transcend, to live out the fullness of a life that resonated with the core of his being. The boundaries of his physical existence felt more confining than ever, a thin veneer over the boundless potential of his dreamscape.

When he finally succumbed to sleep that fateful night, Alistair entered his dream with unusual lucidity, crossing the threshold with an intention forged in the deepest part of his soul. The transition was seamless, the colours, sounds, and textures of the dream world enveloping him as though welcoming him home. He was no longer merely an observer of this reality; he was a participant, heart and soul intertwined with those he loved most.

In this vibrant realm, life with Amelie unfolded in richness and complexity, each day an echo of joy and purpose. Their son grew tall and strong, inheriting his mother's wisdom and his father's insatiable curiosity. The tribe thrived, and with Amelie by his side, Alistair found fulfilment beyond anything he'd known: teaching, learning, and participating in the intricate dance of communal life. The passage of time here was marked not by the ticking of clocks but by the rhythms of nature, the cycles of planting and harvest, life and renewal.

The years flowed by until their son neared his 25th birthday—a significant milestone heralded by an ancient and sacred tradition. As the day approached, Alistair became aware of a calling, a deep spiritual pull that guided him towards an understanding that his integration into this reality demanded a final, transformative act. The tribe prepared for an ancestral ceremony, one that symbolised renewal and prosperity, rooted in the practice of sacrifice, a custom intricately linked to their cultural essence.

Alistair, seeing the unwavering trust and love reflected in the eyes of the tribe, felt a profound sense of peace. He knew this act resonated with the same principles he'd studied as a physician—the sacrifice of self for the greater good, an act of healing and giving. On the appointed day, the tribe gathered under the vast, unwavering gaze of the cosmos. Decorated in the ritualistic regalia of ancient tradition, Alistair stood serenely before the altar, conscious of each breath, each heartbeat.

As the ceremonial chants rose in crescendo, Alistair offered himself willingly, embracing the ethereal transition that would bind his spirit to the prosperity and continuity of the tribe. The act was neither an ending nor a departure; it was a melding with the universe, a transcendence beyond bodily limitations into a state of profound unity with his dream reality.

In the waking world, as Alistair's heart beat its final rhythm on his library sofa, his face bore a gentle expression, hinting at the fulfilment of a lifelong quest realised within the realms of his perception. His journey ended as it had been meant to: a passage not into the void, but into the essence of the life he had chosen, forever integrated with the dreams he cherished.

In the muted silence of Alistair's library, where countless hours had been spent in contemplation and research, the dim light cast gentle shadows that flickered like echoes of the past. The room was filled with the essence of him—books once passionately consulted lay spread across the desk, notes scribbled with reflections on consciousness and reality amassed in towering piles. This space, once vibrant with his intellectual fervour, now cradled his still body as it succumbed to the long-dormant turmoil that had finally risen to claim him.

Alistair's heart, once a vessel of indomitable curiosity and dreams, faltered under the weight of relentless obsession and emotional strain. As he lay on his favourite leather sofa, deep within a dream of his ultimate sacrifice—a sacrifice that bound him eternally to the world he cherished—his physical self quietly disengaged from earthly binds. The transition was serene, unmarked by struggle, as if he'd slipped seamlessly from one reality into another. His face, often clouded with concern and intensity, now radiated a calm acceptance, serene in the possibility of reunion with Amelie and their son.

As the dawn broke, bathing the library in its golden embrace, a different scene unfolded elsewhere, within the halls of academia where Alistair had left an indelible mark. News of his untimely passing spread quickly among his colleagues and students, casting a sombre veil over those who had known him, learned from him, and worked alongside him.

The initial shock of Alistair's death soon gave way to an introspective wave among those he left behind. In faculty lounges and lecture halls, whispers rose—conversations shaped by the haunting knowledge of his profound obsession and the mysterious path he had pursued. Colleagues who had once marvelled at his insights and envied his intellectual rigour were now compelled to delve into his body of work through a new lens, one coloured by his final, intimate journey.

Students, who had been inspired by Alistair's lectures—though often perplexed by the increasingly existential nature of his teachings—began to reexamine the principles he espoused. They pondered over syllabi marked by annotations and lectures punctuated by speeches on interconnected realities and consciousness. Alistair's questions about the very nature of reality lingered, whispered among them as they walked through campus gateways to futures yet forged.

In the ensuing months, Alistair's influence blossomed into a broader conversation, compelling scholarly circles to grapple with the boundaries between the conscious and subconscious, reality and perception. Conferences sparked debates over the implications of his theories, provoking dialogue on the potential for dreams as alternate dimensions or realities. A symposium was dedicated to his memory, intended not only to honour his legacy but to propel further inquiry into the mysterious realms he so passionately explored.

While the world may have lost Alistair Grant, the reverberations of his work and his insatiable quest for understanding ignited a continuing journey of discovery—a journey inspiring others to traverse untrodden paths in pursuit of the timeless mysteries of human consciousness. This legacy, unfettered by his physical absence, would endure, inviting all who dared to ask: what lies beyond the dreams we dream, and could the life within them ever be more real than the one we live?

A QUEST FOR METAMORPHOSIS

Dr. Alan Pierce stood at the window of his spacious office, perched high above the bustling streets of Cambridge. The view, though usually invigorating, barely penetrated his consciousness today. His mind was miles away, traversing the dense canopies of the Amazon rainforest. As a leading psychiatrist at a prestigious university, Alan had spent decades probing the intricacies of the human mind. Yet, it was his unyielding curiosity about the edges of consciousness that distinguished him from his peers.

Alan's journey into the realm of unconventional therapies began early in his career. At a time when electroconvulsive therapy was being reinvigorated, and mindfulness was only just entering the public lexicon, Alan ventured further, intrigued by the transformative power of altered states. A constant companion in his study was "The Psychedelic Handbook: A Practical Guide to Psilocybin, LSD, Ketamine, MDMA, and Ayahuasca". His colleagues often viewed him with a blend of admiration and scepticism, labelling him as both a visionary and a maverick. Undeterred, Alan sought to understand the profound shifts in awareness that could occur beyond the traditional therapeutic spectrum. He was a regular participant in seminars and workshops conducted by State University of Campinas, Brazil.

His interest in this field was not purely academic; it was personal. Years ago, a close encounter with mortality had left an indelible mark on him. A near-fatal car accident had plunged him into a twilight state, a place where time dilated and reality blurred. During those moments suspended between consciousness and oblivion, Alan had experienced a profound clarity—a sense of interconnectedness that conventional medicine could not explain. It was this experience that kindled his enduring fascination with consciousness, urging him to explore the esoteric paths less travelled by his peers.

Among these esoteric paths was his latest and most daring project: the study of rare Amazonian mushrooms reputed to enhance psychic abilities. These fungi, whispered about in shamanic circles as "the gateways to the soul," were said to unlock latent telepathic powers, granting users access to the deepest recesses of the collective unconscious. For Alan, the implications were staggering. The potential to communicate empathically, to perceive thoughts and emotions directly, promised a revolution in therapeutic practices that could transcend the limitations of traditional psychiatry.

In the months preceding this project, Alan had collaborated with ethnobotanists and local shamans, navigating cultural and scientific landscapes to gain permission to study the mushrooms in situ. His efforts culminated in a breakthrough: a colleague's courageous fieldwork had secured a sample of these elusive fungi, setting Alan's research into motion.

He turned away from the window, his gaze settling on the small, locked cabinet across the room. Inside were the precious samples—earthy, unassuming fragments of an organism that could redefine human understanding. Yet, the mushrooms represented more than just a scientific curiosity; they were a bridge to a world where consciousness was expansive and undivided.

As he considered the journey ahead, Alan was acutely aware of the controversy that loomed. The academic community, already divided over his unconventional methods, would scrutinise his every move. Ethical boundaries would be evaluated, as would the very fabric of societal norms regarding human cognition.

Alan returned to his desk, flipping through his meticulously kept notebook. Each page was filled with hypotheses, potential methodologies, and ethical considerations. His heart raced with the anticipation of new discoveries and the promise of understanding the mysterious phenomenon that had once touched him so deeply.

He knew the path he had chosen was fraught with challenges, possibly even peril. Yet, for Dr. Alan Pierce, the allure of the unknown—the possibility of tapping into enhanced consciousness and reshaping the future of psychiatry—was a call too compelling to resist. As twilight settled outside, casting long shadows across his office, Alan felt the weight of his responsibilities and the thrill of uncharted territories that beckoned.

The ordinary Tuesday morning unfurled with an air of expectation for Dr. Alan Pierce. The sunlight barely filtered through the drizzle, casting a silvery hue over the campus.

Alan sat at his mahogany desk, the scent of books and polished wood filling the air when a soft chime interrupted his thoughts. The intercom crackled to life, announcing the arrival of a package at the front desk with his name marked for priority.

Making his way down the echoing corridors of the university, Alan felt an unfamiliar flutter of anticipation. Each footstep seemed to beat in time with his heart as he pondered the potentialities waiting within the package. The building hummed with the steady flow of academia, filled with the murmurs of students and the pages of history unfurling in lecture halls. Yet, for Alan, this particular Tuesday was about the future, not the past.

Arriving at the front desk, he was met with the sight of his long-expected parcel—a plain, nondescript box, its weight suggesting something of substance inside. Alan thanked the receptionist, his fingers almost trembling as they traced the edges of the tape securing the box. As he walked back to his office, the world outside seemed to slip into the background—a mere whisper of reality overshadowed by the promise of discovery nestled beneath cardboard.

Once inside his study, Alan placed the package gently onto his desk. His office, usually a sanctuary of order and calm, now felt alive with potential energy. He took a moment to ground himself, to acknowledge the magnitude of what he held. The mushrooms inside were the culmination of over a year's worth of networking, collaboration, and trust-building with researchers and Indigenous experts far from his ivory tower.

With careful precision, Alan retrieved a letter opener from his desk drawer and sliced through the tape sealing the box. The flaps sprang open, revealing layers of protective padding. Nestled among them were several vacuum-sealed pouches, each containing the rare Amazonian mushrooms he had longed to study. Revered by local shamans, these mushrooms were said to possess powerful psychoactive properties capable of unlocking untapped psychic abilities.

Handling the pouches with a careful reverence usually reserved for priceless artefacts, Alan felt an unanticipated warmth emanating from within. His skin tingled as he delicately lifted a pouch, his mind swirling with possibilities. At that moment, a sudden and vivid flash of perception struck him—a mosaic of foreign thoughts and feelings cascading through his consciousness.

Alan staggered slightly, bracing himself against his desk. In that fleeting heartbeat of time, he glimpsed fragmented images and words—his fellow researcher in the Amazon laughing with guides, a sense of eagerness, and a brief flicker of concern about the mushrooms' potency. The connection faded as swiftly as it had arisen, leaving Alan's heart pounding in the aftermath of what he instinctively recognised as a telepathic experience.

He stood in stunned silence, grappling with the ethereal threads that had just woven through his mind. The vividness of the connection unsettled him, but more than that, it ignited a fierce curiosity. Here was empirical evidence, albeit anecdotal, of the mushrooms' potential—proof that transcended the boundaries of theoretical conjecture.

Could it be that the mushrooms had catalysed this moment of clarity between minds? The notion danced on the edge of plausibility, alternating between exhilarating and terrifying. Driven by the ancient quest for knowledge and buoyed by the thrill of discovery, Alan resolved to understand the phenomena from within.

The decision to conduct a self-experiment was both bold and fraught with risk, yet Alan's penchant for pushing boundaries overshadowed such concerns. In his mind, this was a rare opportunity not to be squandered on academic trepidation. The temptation was too keen, the need for understanding too profound.

Over the following days, Alan meticulously prepared for the experiment within his controlled laboratory environment. He documented his baseline psychological state, subjected himself to various tests, and set up monitoring equipment to ensure safety. Ethical considerations were carefully weighed, though interpreted through a liberally scientific lens.

On the day of the self-experiment, Alan sat alone in his lab, surrounded by the whirring of machines and the sterile comfort of clinical anticipation. Alan had always been fascinated by the layers of the human psyche, the delicate interplay between consciousness and the subconscious. As a psychiatrist, he had devoted his life to understanding the intricate mechanisms that governed thoughts, behaviours, and emotions. Yet, standing in his dimly lit study, he could not shake the feeling that there was more to explore than what his textbooks offered. A profound yearning drew him toward the mysteries hidden within the depths of his own mind.

With a meticulousness borne from years in academia, Alan prepared the Amazonian mushrooms that lay upon his desk. They were a vibrant blend of colours—deep greens, earthy browns, and hints of gold—each one a testament to nature's artistry. He had read tales of their hallucinogenic properties, stories of those who had journeyed into realms of consciousness previously unfathomed. With trepidation, he gazed at the fungi, pondering the potential consequences of this undertaking.

The legends spoke of transformation. Alan recalled the myth of the Ouroboros, the serpent devouring its own tail, symbolizing the cyclical nature of life, death, and rebirth. The parallels between the snake and his own desires for growth felt inescapable. As a child, he had often been enamoured with the concept of metamorphosis—the idea that one could shed the constraints of the past to emerge anew. He saw the act of consuming these mushrooms as a gateway to that very rebirth.

As the first wave of the mushrooms worked their magic, reality began to thin around him. Colours intensified, and the very fabric of his thoughts started to unravel. Ancient symbols danced before his eyes—mythological archetypes from lost civilizations, each one beckoning him to explore the layers of his own unconscious. The deeper he ventured, the more he felt himself slipping into an alternate reality, one where the boundaries of his human experience blurred against the backdrop of something grander.

Visions came flooding in: serpents coiling around pillars of stone, echoing their wisdom in the chambers of his mind. The trickster archetype—playful yet profound—appeared first to nudge him deeper into the abyss of his own psyche. "Embrace your shadows," it seemed to whisper, an invitation wrapped in riddles. Alan felt the rush of his heart, uncertainty mingling with exhilaration. He had spent years guiding his patients through their own darkness; perhaps it was time to confront his.

Then came the Anima, an ethereal figure embodying both beauty and terror. She danced through visions of ancient forests, her serpentine grace captivating yet ominous. Each movement resonated with a deep understanding of transformation. Alan watched, spellbound, as the snake's symbolism unfolded: its ability to shed skin and emerge renewed, overcoming the limitations of its prior form. It tugged at a deep part of him, reminding him of the countless times he had chosen to remain stagnant, entrapped by fear.

As the sensory overload peaked, something within him began to break free. The feeling was not merely psychological but profoundly physical. He felt the tightening of his own skin, as if it had become a shroud that weighed him down, ready to be cast aside. The boundaries of his physical identity shattered, revealing something beyond mere flesh and bone.

In that moment, Alan experienced a cosmic realization. Quantum physics whispered truths of multiple realities—the Evertonian Many Worlds Interpretation—the knowledge that every decision branched off into an alternate dimension where different versions of oneself existed. Each choice, every fear, laid rippling paths of existence that he could explore. Could he not also become these other selves? Could he not embrace the serpent within?

With that thought, the metamorphosis began. The shedding of his skin was both painful and liberating, as he felt limbs contorting and reshaping, the space around him warping to accommodate the new essence emerging from within. His fingers elongated, becoming sleek and scaled. A shiver coursed through him, igniting a flame of instinctual understanding where intellect had once ruled.

He opened his eyes—and they had multiplied, each a reflective orb that caught the light with predatory sharpness. His new vision was acute, allowing him to see beyond the mere physical realm. The world shimmered, revealing layers of energy and consciousness interwoven with the fabric of existence. The colours were vibrant, alive with the pulse of the universe.

Yet even as he revelled in his newfound form, fragments of his human mind struggled against this primal identity. The conflict waged inside him, a juxtaposition of the intellectual man he had been and the instinctual creature he was becoming. Each thought felt like a distant echo, muffled by the throbbing awareness of his multi-hooded reality. Dr. Alan Pierce, once a man of reason and logic, was now something more complex—an embodiment of ancient wisdom and primal instincts, merging into a singular consciousness.

As he slithered along the floor, the sensations were both foreign and exhilarating. His new body moved with an elegance that transcended human experience; he felt the floor against his scales, the vibrations of the world coursing through him. The air was an intoxicating mélange of scents—earthy, alive, and pulsing with energy.

He found himself drawn to the mirror in the corner of the study, the glass now reflecting not just a man but a creature of legend. Multi-hued hoods crowned his head, each one symbolic of a different aspect of his psyche. They swayed independently, each symbolizing a fragment of his identity—the scientist, the patient healer, the seeker of truth. This transformation was not merely cosmetic; it was an integration of all the selves that had existed within him, now emerging as one.

In that moment, he realized he stood at the crossroads of realities, his journey intertwined with the echoes of countless choices across the multiverse. He was both Alan Pierce and something ancient, something wise—a manifestation of archetypes that had guided humanity through ages, the serpent representing the wound and its healing.

With newfound purpose, Alan instinctively navigated through his home, the familiar boundaries now expansive and fluid. Every corner called to him, every shadow whispered secrets of the unseen. He slipped through the door and into the vibrant, pulsating night.

The world outside was transformed in his eyes. The streets, once mere roads of asphalt, now appeared as flowing riverbeds, shimmering with stories and energies. The moon above cast ethereal light, filtering through the canopy of trees like a gentle caress of the cosmos. He could feel the heartbeat of the earth beneath him, each pulse resonating in time with his own, reinforcing the primal connection to life.

As he glided into the depths of the forest bordering his home, every leaf crackled with energy, each whisper of the wind carried ancient truths. Alan sensed the presence of beings woven into the night; shadowy figures enveloped in the rich scenario of existence. The myths spoke of these keepers—guardians of wisdom, ancestors who had once roamed the earth in search of enlightenment. He could almost hear them now, their voices harmonizing with the chorus of the night.

"Become one," a voice echoed within him, urging him to intertwine with the universe. "Explore the many worlds that await your essence."

He dove deeper into the woods, the dance of foliage guiding him toward a clearing bathed in moonlight. It was here that the veil between worlds felt thinnest. As he coiled among the roots of ancient trees, he felt a pull—a gravitational force inviting him to reach beyond the constraints of his physical form and to experiment with the parallel realities laid before him.

With an intense focus, he closed his eyes, allowing the energy of the universe to envelop him. The sensation was like falling through an infinite tunnel, where moments and potential futures flitted past him in vibrant colours. Each represented a different choice, a decision that could alter the course of his life. Alan felt both empowered and bewildered, the weight of his own existence pressing against the threshold of understanding.

He explored each reality, experiencing the multitude of paths he could have taken, paralleled by his journey as a serpent—whether to protect, to transcend, to heal, or to challenge the status quo. In one reality, he saw himself as a revered sage, teaching the secrets of the mind to those eager to learn. In another, he grappled with darker impulses, becoming a being lost to fear and regret. Each possibility fed into the mosaic of his identity, revealing truths he had long shied away from.

Each choice birthed a serpent within him, an aspect of self that called for acknowledgment. As he shed his old skin, it became clear that rebirth was not merely shedding what had come before but embracing every facet of existence—both light and dark. He was the Ouroboros of his own journey: the beginning, the end, and the continuum of possibilities.

Yet, with this knowledge also came a visceral confrontation with his greatest fears. He witnessed his human anxieties come alive—the fear of inadequacy, the dread of failure—but in his serpent form, they lost their grip on him. They shifted into shadows that darted at the periphery, dissolving into the night rather than imprisoning him.

As the night deepened, a reckoning awaited. The voices of the ancestors surged alongside him, beckoning him to face his ultimate truth. They whispered of sacrifice and legacy, of the bridges between worlds and the scars left by decisions yet to be made. This was not merely about knowing oneself; it was about navigating the labyrinth of interconnected lives that each individual embodied across various dimensions. In this realm of multiverses, every aspect of himself—every choice, every fear—came to a head as wisdom gathered within him, coalescing into a single, powerful vortex of clarity.

Alan found himself in a place he had never quite anticipated: the crossroads not just of reality, but of identity. Here, in the sacred clearing wrapped in moonlight, he was called to confront the foundational truths about who he was and what he might become. No longer was he solely Dr. Alan Pierce, a psychiatrist ensnared in the confines of human limitations; now he was a vessel of infinite possibility, an embodiment of the serpent's wisdom—the fertility of beginnings and ends intertwined.

He sensed a presence then, a guardian emerging from the shadows of the trees—the shape of a majestic serpent, larger than any he had seen. Its scales shimmered with an otherworldly glow, reflecting hues of emerald, green, sapphire blue, and hints of gold that danced in the moonlight. As it approached, Alan felt an overwhelming sense of connection and reverence. This was a being of ancient knowledge, a keeper of the thresholds between worlds.

The serpent lowered its head, and with an uncanny gentleness, it allowed its gaze to meet Alan's myriad eyes. In that moment, he was flooded with visions of the world as the serpent understood it—a realm of cycles and truths that transcended the simplistic narrative of good and evil, success and failure. The serpent's wisdom spoke of balance, of the necessity of embracing both sides of the coin to truly understand one's path.

"You have journeyed far, Dr. Pierce," the serpent's voice resonated within him, reverberating through the very marrow of his core. "What have you discovered in shedding the limitations of your human form?"

"I have found that every choice carries its weight," Alan replied, his voice echoing in a harmonious blend of human thought and serpentine instinct. "I see the glimmers of potential, but I fear the darkness intertwined in each path I could take."

"Fear is a kind of skin we wear," the serpent explained, coiling closer, its eyes swirling with ancient knowledge. "But in shedding that skin, you allow room for growth. The fear will always be present, but you must see it as a part of your journey, one that offers insight rather than constraint."

With each word spoken, Alan felt the serpent's wisdom seep into him, unravelling the threads of anxiety he had held onto so closely. There was liberation in understanding that fear itself was not an enemy but a teacher—an essential guide through the shadowy corners of existence. The journey ahead would not be without its challenges; he knew that now. But armed with this knowledge, he would learn to navigate those complexities with grace.

"In this form, you possess the power to transcend," the serpent continued. "You are not only experiencing life but influencing it—a reflection of the Many Worlds. Each choice you make resonates in parallel dimensions, shaping the realities of those around you."

A profound revelation began to bloom within his mind. Alan felt his consciousness stretching into the infinite expanses of potential. He could choose to weave his new form into the fabric of existence, becoming a force that influenced growth, healing, and understanding in ways that surpassed his previous experiences as a human.

"Now, it is time for you to return," the serpent said, its presence commanding yet soothing. "The world needs your insights, your gifts. The dance of life continues, and you hold the keys to unlock awareness in others."

In an instant, he could see the interconnectedness of everything—the web of life woven intricately around him, forming pathways that could alter the very course of history. How many lives could be uplifted through understanding? How many fears transformed into wisdom?

"I will remember," Alan pledged, knowing that within him lay endless reservoirs of experience and knowledge yet untapped. "I will embrace this duality—the human and the serpent."

As dawn began to break, casting a soft glow across the forest, he felt the pull of reality tightening around him. The colours of the world began to solidify, the vibrant tones softening into the reassuring hues of the morning. It was time to return to his human form, yet he knew he could never go back to the man he had been. The truths he had discovered would forever shape his existence.

With a gentle exhale, Alan allowed himself to flow through the dimensions, shedding his serpentine body as one sheds winter's coat in springtime. The transition was effortless, a merging of selves rather than a sacrifice of one for the other. He felt himself shifting and transforming, each scale retreating, each hood fading as he embraced the embodiment of Dr. Alan Pierce once more.

The metamorphosis concluded as he awoke in his familiar study, the early light filtering in through the window, casting golden rays upon the dusty books stacked high. He regained his human form, yet the essence of the serpent lingered within him, entwined with every fibre of his being. Stretching his limbs, Alan took a moment to absorb the reality of his surroundings, holding tightly to the memory of his transformation. He could feel the echo of the ancient wisdom pulsing beneath his skin, like an underlying rhythm that synchronized with the very essence of the universe.

Sitting upright, he allowed the dawn's light to wash over him, igniting his thoughts and igniting a fire within his soul. Consciousness had taken on richer hues, exhibiting the myriad shades of understanding that had been gifted to him in the forest. The serpent's insight still thrummed in his heart—each experience across the dimensions was interwoven into the very fabric of being, every choice an opportunity for growth.

As the morning unfolded, Alan's mind raced with possibilities. He recognized that he would no longer be merely a psychiatrist confined to the walls of his office. His experiences, both as man and serpent, had opened new vistas of understanding, not only for himself but for those who found their way into his practice. He would guide his patients not just as a healer, but as a mentor who had navigated the labyrinth of consciousness and emerged with revelations.

Harnessing the energy of his transformation, Alan began to write. He poured his experiences onto the page with fervour, each word an invocation of the wisdom he had channelled during his encounter with the serpent. He scribbled visions of the multiverse, threading them into narratives that merged mythology and cognitive science. Each sentence served as both a personal testament and a guidepost for others to seek their own truth.

As he wrote, the shadows of his previous fears and doubts were diminished, the darkness transformed into understanding. He drafted new frameworks for therapy that incorporated the exploration of the self through varied dimensions and perspectives, encouraging his patients to embrace the multifaceted aspects of their identity. They could learn to dance with their fears instead of succumbing to them — to understand that every choice and alteration shaped the paths before them.

Days turned into weeks, and as he shared his newfound therapeutic techniques with patients, he saw real transformations taking shape. Individuals who had previously felt trapped in cycles of despair and confusion began to awaken. They, too, were shedding their skins, discovering latent parts of themselves yearning to emerge. The results were astonishing; healing blossomed before his eyes, entwined with the very essence of ancient wisdom that had graced him.

Among those who came to him was Sarah—a woman whose past was marked by trauma, leaving her adrift in a sea of anxiety and depression. With an open heart, she entered Alan's office, her spirit fragile yet resilient. Remembering the serpent's wisdom, he guided her through her own journey of transformation. In their sessions, he encouraged her to envision herself as a creature capable of renewal, teaching her to articulate her fears while inviting her to embrace the journey rather than resist it.

"Imagine shedding your old skin," Alan suggested one afternoon, as he shared stories of his own transformation. "What might that feel like? What would you do differently if you were free from the weight of your past?"

As Sarah closed her eyes, Alan watched her expression shift. In that moment, a glimmer of understanding broke through, manifested in the tiny smile that began to grace her lips. The journey of illuminating the paths of her consciousness had begun, and Alan felt honoured to be a part of her metamorphosis.

The word began to spread. Whispers of the new methods Alan had embraced began to ripple through the broader community; sceptics turned believers as they witnessed the power of self-discovery. He created workshops and retreat spaces, inviting seekers to explore their psyches within the ancient wisdom of mythology, cognitive science, and the art of transformation, much like he had experienced with the serpent.

But as Alan immersed himself in guiding others, he remained ever mindful of the serpent's timeless lesson: true transformation must be accompanied by introspection. Though he felt the rhythm of fulfilment in helping others, he knew the journey was ongoing. His own fears needed tending, too—principally the fear of losing the essence of the serpent within him. It was not just a transformation but an everyday practice of acknowledging that both his human vulnerabilities and serpentine wisdom were essential to his identity.

One evening, as he stood in the forest clearing again— the very place where his initial transformation had struck him with raw energy—the shadows of dusk enveloped him. He closed his eyes and recalled the experience of merging with the serpent. In the stillness, he allowed himself to take in the myriad dimensions around him, feeling the energy vibrate through the roots of ancient trees and the whispering winds.

"Serpent," he called gently, honouring the bond that had been forged. "I seek your guidance once more."

The air shimmered, and the same majestic serpent appeared before him, its presence imbued with a sense of knowing. "You have thrived in your journey, Alan. What brings you here?"

"I fear losing the essence of the truth I have gained," Alan confessed, his voice carrying the weight of introspection. "In my efforts to guide others, I worry that I may forget the lessons I have learned—the wisdom of transformation and the power of embracing both light and shadow."

The serpent regarded him with wise, perceptive eyes, and for a moment, they simply existed in silence, sharing the sacred space between man and creature. Alan felt the connection, not merely as a memory of his past metamorphosis, but as an ongoing relationship that was dynamic and alive—a continual call to evolve.

"Transformation is not a singular event," the serpent spoke softly, its words rippling through Alan's consciousness, resonating deeply. "It is a series of ongoing awakenings. The journey never truly ends; with each challenge you face, another layer peels away. Your fears and wisdom will always coexist within you and recognizing them is where true power lies."

With those words, clarity washed over Alan. He understood now that the balance he sought was not just about using his experiences to guide others; it was also about honouring his ongoing evolution. Each moment of fear or doubt was merely a reminder of a lesson still in progress. The key was to integrate those experiences into his identity rather than dismiss them.

"Remember this," the serpent continued, undulating gracefully in the moonlight. "Your form will shift, not only physically but also in how you perceive your place in the multiverse. Embrace each state—you are the student and the teacher, the seeker and the sage."

Alan nodded, feeling a surge of purpose envelop him. "I will embrace the entirety of my existence, acknowledging every part of myself—the fears, the shadows, the wisdom. I will integrate them into my work and continue guiding others through their own journeys. I promise to keep the lessons of transformation alive within me."

As morning began to break—the soft hues of dawn weaving their way through the canopy—he felt a shift within, something that had settled deeply into his core. The serpent's presence brought a sense of calm empowerment, a reminder that metamorphosis is a continuous act of creation. With gratitude flowing from him, Alan understood this bond extended beyond mere guidance; it was an alliance of consciousness, one that invited exploration, curiosity, and deeper understanding.

"I thank you, great serpent, for your wisdom and for guiding my journey," he said, his heart filled with reverence.

The serpent inclined its head, its scales shimmering like stars against a velvety sky. "You are never alone in your journey, Alan. Trust in your path and the connections you forge. You will find that the universe will always reflect back what you seek to understand."

With that, a sense of belonging enveloped him, and as the light of day broke through fully, illuminating the transforming world around him, Alan knew he was prepared to embrace whatever awaited him. The lessons of his transformation flowed seamlessly into the everyday, illuminating the darkest corners of his understanding.

Back in his practice, Alan incorporated the idea of multidimensional awareness into his sessions, presenting the concept of alternate selves to his patients. He encouraged them to explore their multifaceted identities, diving into the depths of their fears, dreams, and dormant potentials with the understanding that they too were capable of shedding their skins. The therapeutic space became a haven of transformation, where individuals were invited to honour their unique journeys.

As he continued to guide others, Alan felt empowered by the stories that emerged—the triumphs of transformation and self-discovery intertwined in the narratives of those he helped. Each success story illuminated a piece of his own healing, serving as a reminder that even in moments of doubt, growth was always possible.

As months sped by, Alan found himself immersed not only in therapy but also in writing. He began assembling his insights and experiences into a comprehensive guide that blended cognitive science with the ancient wisdom he had encountered in his serpentine journey. His book, aptly titled *The Serpent Within: Embracing Transformation Through Ancient Wisdom*, sought to offer pathways for anyone seeking to understand the concept of metamorphosis beyond superficial change, celebrating the darker aspects of existence alongside the brightness.

The day of its release arrived, and Alan stood in front of a gathering of eager faces in a local community centre—his heart swelling with both excitement and nerves. He had invited previous patients, colleagues, and community members, all gathered to share in this milestone of not just his work, but their collective growth and healing journeys.

"I stand here before you," he began, his voice steady yet imbued with emotion, "not just as Dr. Alan Pierce, but as someone who has walked through the fires of transformation and emerged with wisdom that is as much yours as it is mine. We all have our fears and shadows, but it's in facing them that we begin to understand our true selves."

He shared anecdotes from his practice, intertwined with the lessons of the serpent and the profound realization of interconnectedness. The audience hung onto his every word, faces illuminated with recognition and hope.

In the days and weeks following, the feedback poured in from readers and participants in the event. Alan found himself invigorated by their reactions—emails and messages flooded in from people who had resonated with his journey and the transformative ideas he had shared. Individuals who had felt trapped in their own narratives began to express their appreciation, revealing how the lessons from his book had encouraged them to explore the multiple dimensions of their own identities.

Sarah, the woman he had worked with, reached out to share her story. She penned a heartfelt letter detailing how his guidance had steered her through the darkness of her past, empowering her to confront the fears that once paralyzed her. "I feel like a new person," she wrote, "like I've shed the skin of my past self. The serpent's wisdom you shared helped me find the strength to embrace my journey, and for that, I will always be grateful."

As Alan absorbed the impact of his work, he realized he needed to incorporate these newfound insights not just into his practice, but into his life as a whole. He consistently reminded himself of the serpent's teachings, often returning to the forest clearing where everything had begun, allowing nature to recalibrate his awareness and guide his spirit.

With each visit to that sacred space, he delved deeper into his own consciousness, reflecting on the lessons learned and the endless possibilities of transformation. The woods whispered around him, a living testament to the cycles of life, offering solace during moments of doubt. Here, he could quiet his busy thoughts and reconnect with the snake within, reminding him of the dualities that defined his existence.

One particularly crisp evening, he returned to the clearing. The air was thick with anticipation, a tangible energy that sent ripples of excitement through him. Closing his eyes, he immersed himself in the symphony of the forest—the rustling leaves, the chorus of crickets, and the occasional call of an owl echoing in the distance.

In this meditative state, Alan envisioned the serpent coiling around him once more, its eyes filled with knowing and compassion. "What do you seek tonight, Dr. Pierce?" the serpent inquired, its voice echoing in the depths of his mind.

"I seek to understand how I can continue to grow," Alan replied earnestly, feeling the truth of his words resonate. "I feel the weight of others' expectations, the pressure to maintain the wisdom I've shared. But I fear losing touch with the lessons I've learned along the way."

"Growth is not linear, nor is it static," the serpent responded. "You may never fully embody the wisdom you think you should, but you can embody the journey itself. Allow yourself to be imperfect, to wander. Embrace each moment, for they contribute to your evolution. You remain the seeker, as every transformant must be."

With those words, Alan felt an intimacy with his own vulnerability, the beauty in unknowingness. The idea that he need not have all the answers, that the journey was as valuable as the destination, brought him profound relief. It was a reminder that embracing uncertainty was a fundamental aspect of his human experience—one he had long championed in his practice.

As the evening deepened, he opened his eyes to the myriad stars that now blanketed the night sky, their twinkling light a reflection of countless potential paths stretching infinitely before him. Each star was a reminder that each option had its lessons, its beauty, and its challenges. Instead of feeling overwhelmed, he felt invigorated by the possibilities.

With renewed strength, Alan continued to embrace his transformative journey, both personally and professionally. Over the next year, he expanded his practice, developing workshops that encouraged participants to embrace the unknown within themselves. He called them "Serpent's Path: Embracing Your Infinite Potential," designed to guide others through their own metamorphoses, using meditative practices, storytelling, and deep reflection.

He brought groups into the forest, much like his own journey, allowing the natural world to facilitate their inner exploration. He witnessed transformational moments echo through the lives of those present, as participants confronted their fears, explored their shadows, and ultimately found paths to renewed identities.

Firelight flickered in the evenings as stories were shared, laughter blended with tears, and moments of camaraderie illustrated the powerful connections humans could forge when they acknowledged their shared struggles.

One evening, while gathered around a campfire, Alan looked around at the faces illuminated by the soft glow. There was Sarah, who now radiated confidence; another participant, John, who had struggled with long-buried guilt, and Mia, who had found courage to express herself creatively for the first time in years. They were all in varying stages of their transformations, each representing a different facet of the many worlds Alan had envisioned.

"We are all here," Alan began, his voice steady and warm, "to embrace our true selves. Each of us embarks on a unique journey, yet we do so together. We are not defined by our fears but by the courage we summon to face them. Remember the sacred wisdom of the serpent —embracing the cycles of shedding and renewal. Tonight, let's share our stories; let us remind each other that in vulnerability lies our strength."

As the fire crackled, participants began to share their experiences—some vulnerable, others jubilant, and all rich with the wisdom they had gleaned along the way. Each narrative wove into the scenario of the gathering, creating a sense of unity among the diverse individuals present. As they spoke, Alan watched the transformations unfold before him, realizing the profound impact of community in the journey of self-discovery.

John spoke first; his voice shaky but strong. "Before I came here, I felt trapped in my own mind, haunted by decisions I couldn't forgive. But through this journey, I've discovered that holding onto that guilt only chained me to my past. I've learned to forgive myself, to recognize those mistakes as the foundations of my growth. I can't change what happened, but I can choose how it defines me from here on out."

Mia followed, her face brightening as she shared, "I've always hidden my creativity, convinced it wasn't good enough. This space has taught me to express my art without fear of judgment. I remember the first time I painted here; it was liberating! I poured my heart onto the canvas, and instead of criticism, I found support. That's what we create together—freedom and encouragement."

Each story revealed the intricate layers of humanity, the beauty of transformation wrapped in uncertainty yet threaded with hope. Alan felt the energy shift in the environment, the collective spirit pulsing with resilience. They were all participants in a sacred ritual—the act of unearthing their truths and standing in their authenticity.

As stories flowed into the night, Alan listened intently, taking the time to reflect on the way each person articulated their journey toward understanding. He recognized the significance of their experiences—not only as individuals but also as part of a greater continuum. They were embodying the very essence of the serpent's wisdom, learning to navigate the complexities within and the interconnectedness among themselves.

As the flames flickered lower and the night deepened, a thought occurred to Alan that resonated profoundly: **the journey of metamorphosis is never complete.** It is a continuous cycle of learning, retreating into the shadows to reclaim lost parts of oneself, stepping into the light with renewed courage.

The gathering eventually dispersed, but Alan remained by the dying fire, contemplating the stories shared and the lives touched. Each person carried within them echoes of the serpent's journey—their souls entwined with the symbolism of shedding skins and rebirth.

The weeks that followed solidified Alan's resolve. He began to incorporate more elements from the natural world into his practice, introducing mindfulness practices that encouraged mindfulness and grounding. He saw the healing power of nature as a vital complement to the cognitive work he had championed for so long. The earth was not just external—it was a repository of wisdom and a teacher for those willing to listen.

On particularly beautiful days, he would lead sessions in open fields, alongside gentle streams—encouraging his patients to reconnect with the elements surrounding them. They would ground themselves through breath, become aware of the sensations beneath their feet, and honour the earth that nurtured them. Together, they explored insights that flowed in tandem with the natural rhythms of life.

Yet even as Alan flourished in his work, he remained mindful of the balance between weaving wisdom into his practice and nurturing himself. There were days when self-doubt crept in, shadows of the past threatening to re-emerge. But with each encounter with nature, he found reassurance, allowing himself to experience the duality of existence. The darker feelings were not swept away but welcomed as part of the ever-evolving journey.

One calm afternoon, as Alan sat in a sun-dappled meadow establishing a new workshop, he felt an overwhelming sense of gratitude. The journey had transformed him, guiding him not only to help others but also to embrace his vulnerabilities and bare his soul more than he ever thought possible.

As participants arrived, he greeted them with warmth and openness. "Welcome to our journey together. Today, we'll delve deeper into understanding what it means to shed our skins, to renew ourselves, and to commune with nature. Let's honour the many layers within us, recognizing each as an essential part of who we are."

As the workshop began, he guided the participants through exercises that invited them to explore their inner landscapes. They sat in circles, practiced creative visualization, and engaged with their own metaphorical skins—choosing what they might shed and what new identities they longed to embrace. The experience culminated in storytelling, where each person could voice their renewed intentions, their hopes, and their dreams into the sacred space they had created together.

As twilight approached, and the sun dipped below the horizon, participants began to create lanterns from natural materials, imbuing each one with their affirmations of transformation. It became a ritual, a symbolic manifestation of light igniting in the darkness—reminders of the endless possibilities that lay ahead.

As they completed their lanterns, Alan felt the air thrum with anticipation. When the last lantern was finished, he gathered everyone in a circle, their eyes flickering with excitement and wonder. "Tonight, as we close our gathering, let us release our intentions into the world," he said, his voice steady, carrying a blend of authority and warmth.

One by one, they each shared what their lantern represented: forgiveness, creativity, courage, and renewal. These offerings were more than mere symbols; they were declarations of solidarity with the journey toward transformation, both personal and collective.

"Tonight, we celebrate not only the light within us but also the darkness that has led us here," Alan continued, sensing the significance of their gathering. "Let's remember that both aspects are essential; they complete our existence. When we embrace the shadow, we empower the light."

As dusk settled, Alan led them down a narrow path toward a nearby stream, where the water glistened under the moonlight, captivating in its silvery glow. They stood along the banks, the soothing sounds of the water creating a serene backdrop. Here, they would release the lanterns— each one a manifestation of their intentions, set adrift into the current of the river.

"On the count of three, we'll set our lanterns free," he instructed, a spark of anticipation igniting in the air. "As you release yours, envision it carrying your dreams, hopes, and intentions forth into the universe. Let it be a guide for your own transformation."

"ONE… TWO… THREE!"

With those words, a cascade of light flickered as lanterns floated gently into the water, their soft glow illuminating the dark surface. Each one danced upon the ripples, carrying with it the hopes and stories of those who had crafted them. For Alan, watching the glowing lights drift away stirred a profound sense of belonging—a connection to the greater web of life threading through the universe.

As they stood in silence, watching the lanterns bob along the current, an overwhelming sense of peace enveloped him. In that moment, it became beautifully evident that they were all interconnected: an ensemble of spirits navigating the waters of life, each on their unique journey but bound by a shared experience of exploration and growth.

Days turned into weeks again, and as the seasons shifted, Alan continued to find ways to deepen his practice and enrich the lives of others. He incorporated nature walks, meditation retreats, and creative workshops into his offerings—each session fostering healing, authenticity, and the embrace of one's totality.

Amidst the continued success and transformation, he also personally explored new avenues; he finished writing his book. He felt it was complete—an invitation to readers to venture into the wilderness of their own minds, where they could confront fears, embrace shadows, and emerge renewed.

The book was published and received well, resonating with people from various walks of life. Alan received testimonials from readers whose lives had changed through the teachings he had distilled within its pages; the themes of transformation, acceptance, and interconnectedness echoed across the spectrum of human experience.

He began holding book discussions, creating spaces for dialogue and storytelling among diverse readers. As he listened to their experiences, Alan became even more aware of the varied ways people interpreted themes of metamorphosis. Each insight provided him with fuel for his own growth, illustrating that the journey of transformation was never confined to one perspective—it was as varied as the lives it touched.

One night, while preparing for a discussion, he sat at his desk, reflecting on the paths he had travelled. The tracing of his work with patients, the evolution of his workshops, and the profound connections formed all sprang to life in his mind like constellations in the sky. All these experiences converged into a singular truth: within every person exists the capacity for radical metamorphosis.

As he wrote down thoughts for the upcoming discussion, he felt the gentle tug of the serpent's wisdom at the edges of his consciousness—a reminder that metamorphosis was part of the ongoing cycle, and that he, too, remained a seeker. Life would continue to unveil layers of understanding, and he was not merely a guide but a participant in the unfolding narrative.

As the discussion commenced that evening, the room hummed with energy, filled with a sense of community that warmly embraced every individual. Alan welcomed participants and opened the space for conversation. "Each of us carries a unique story—a narrative that reflects not just who we were, but who we aspire to be. Let's share our tales tonight, and together, tap into the richness of our collective experiences."

The room swirled with voices as people shared moments of vulnerability and strength. A reader spoke of chapter 2's lesson on enveloping darkness, recalling how relinquishing his fears had empowered him to navigate relationships with newfound empathy. Another recounted how discovering her own creativity had rekindled her sense of self, allowing her to approach life with a zest previously absent.

As the stories unfolded, Alan led them deeper into the labyrinth of their transformative experiences, encouraging each participant to dig further into their journeys, drawing connections between their personal metamorphoses and the universal themes outlined in his book.

"Transformation," Alan reminded them gently, "is not merely an endpoint; it is a continual cycle, much like the seasons. Each story we share, each lesson we glean from our experiences, nourishes us as we shed old layers and emerge renewed. Like the serpent, we must embrace the shedding process, for that is where the true magic lies."

The energy in the room shifted, and participants leaned forward, intrigued by the invitation to explore the deeper relevance of their experiences. A woman in the back spoke up, her voice quivering with emotion. "I've felt so lost since the loss of my father last year. I thought I could never find myself again. But your book prompted me to explore my grief, allowing it to transform into something that honours his memory. That darkness can be a guide, and I'm learning to navigate it differently."

Murmurs of acknowledgment rippled through the circle, and Alan felt a profound sense of gratitude for the authenticity displayed. Here, in this moment, everyone was participating in the ongoing dance of transformation, where vulnerability became a source of strength rather than a burden.

Another participant, a young man named Liam, shared how the concept of the multidimensional self-resonated with him deeply. "When I embraced the idea that I could explore different versions of myself, I realized I wasn't confined to who I was expected to be. I could dream bigger—I could become who I truly am. I'm creating art and pursuing a career in music now because I've allowed myself to shed those limiting beliefs."

Alan watched in awe as the stories weaved together, interconnected in a way that encapsulated the essence of the workshop: each voice complementing the others, creating a feedback loop of encouragement and support. They reflected each other's growth—a scenario of shared humanity.

As the discussion continued, Alan felt more than ever that he was both a part of this community and a facilitator of their collective journey. Their stories were echoes of his own, reminding him that transformation is a shared experience, a gentle reminder of life's cyclical nature.

When the evening drew to a close, and participants began to depart, Alan lingered for a moment, leaning against the wall as he watched them leave. Their faces—each telling a story of its own—were a reminder of the profound impact shared narratives can have. He felt a renewed sense of purpose, for they had all joined in a sacred act of exchange, where their lives began to shimmer with the threads of possibility.

Over the next few months, the success of his book propelled him further into the spotlight. He was invited to speak at conferences and workshops, his transformative message receiving national attention. Each opportunity brought the chance to share his journey and the rich narratives of others who dared to embrace their own metamorphoses.

As he stepped into these settings, he felt the familiar tug of the serpent within—a reminder of the ongoing journey. No matter the accolades or success, he remained a seeker, deeply aware of the lessons still to be learned.

During one speaking engagement, held in a grand auditorium filled with eager faces, Alan took a breath and stepped onto the stage. The excitement in the air was palpable, and he scanned the audience, each person representing a unique story waiting to be unveiled. "It is a pleasure to be here," he began, his voice steady, tinged with passion. "Today, we will explore the art of transformation, not as a destination but as an ever-evolving process."

He spoke about shedding old layers, embracing fears, and nurturing the interconnectedness between individuals as they navigate the uncertainties of life. Alan drew from personal stories, weaving them alongside anecdotes from patients who had found their own paths of healing. He shared the wisdom gleaned from the serpent and the transformative experiences that shaped him.

That day, Alan learned just as much from those in attendance as they might learn from him. Their questions sparked deep discussions about resilience, growth, and the nature of suffering as a catalyst for transformation. He saw reflected in their eyes a collective understanding that life is nothing if not an intricate dance of shedding, growing, and renewing.

As months turned into years, he continued to foster these connections—life became a series of interactions intertwining stories of struggle and triumph. Through retreats and workshops, his community blossomed, each gathering fostering deeper understandings of the self and the myriad paths of existence.

One spring afternoon, while leading a workshop in the woods, Alan stood in a clearing surrounded by familiar faces. The sun peeked through the treetops in a stunning display of light and warmth. He began the session, "Today, we return to nature, the source of our deepest inspirations. It teaches us that transformation is woven into the very fabric of existence."

As participants engaged with the natural surroundings, Alan felt the familiar serpent energy guiding them through explorative exercises that honoured their individual and shared journeys. They created artistic expressions inspired by their experiences, using nature's materials—twigs, leaves, and stones. Each participant channelled their emotions into these creations, embodying the essence of renewal and transformation.

"Remember," Alan encouraged as they worked, "nature thrives on cycles. Just as a tree sheds its leaves in autumn to prepare for new growth in spring, we too can let go of what no longer serves us and make space for fresh beginnings."

He moved among the participants, observing as they connected with the earth and with each other. Laughter and conversation filled the air—a testament to the nurturing atmosphere they had cultivated together. The essence of the serpent resonated within them, reminding them of their interconnectedness and the beauty of the metamorphosis they all shared.

As the afternoon wore on, Alan invited them to share their creations with the group. One by one, participants stood up, revealing their artistic expressions. A woman—Jasmine—held up a delicate sculpture made of intertwined branches and blossoms. "This represents the intertwining of my fears and hopes. I am learning to embrace both; they are parts of who I am."

Another participant, Peter, shared a mandala formed from various stones he had found nearby. "This mandala symbolizes my journey. Each stone represents a different phase I've gone through—some heavy and burdensome, others light and freeing. By placing them in this circle, I acknowledge every part of my transformation."

As stories flowed, Alan could feel the room pulsing with energy—a celebration of vulnerability and authenticity, each story echoing the others, illuminating the complexities of their existence while embedding them within the healing power of community.

The sun was beginning to set, casting a golden hue across the clearing when he invited everyone to participate in a closing ceremony. "Let's reflect on our experiences today and what we each wish to carry forward," he said. "Take a moment to think of one lesson you've gained, one intention you wish to honour as we step back into our lives."

They formed a circle, and Alan invited each person to share their intention. As they went around the circle, powerful affirmations emerged, underscoring the strength found in connection—each person voicing their aspirations, from committing to creativity to embracing vulnerability, nurturing relationships, or fostering self-love.

As the last intention was shared, Alan felt a profound sense of accomplishment swell within him. This workshop, once just an idea sparked by his own transformation, had become a powerful gathering space for others seeking their paths. What began as his journey had shifted into a collective odyssey; he was no longer just a guide, but a participant in the shared medicinal experience of life.

Feeling the weight of gratitude, he raised his voice softly. "Let's close our time together with a moment of silence—not just for reflection, but to honour the journeys we are all on together. Let this silence be a space for growth, healing, and acknowledgment of our interconnected journeys."

The group fell silent, the only sounds breaking the tranquillity being the whispers of the trees and the gentle rustle of leaves in the cool evening breeze. In that moment, Alan envisioned the threads of their stories intertwining, echoing the eternal dance of transformation and renewal.

As the sun dipped below the horizon, casting hues of orange, pink, and purple across the sky, the group embraced the moment, absorbing the beauty of nature wrapping around them. There was an unspoken understanding that each of them carried a part of one another, a piece of wisdom rooted in their experiences shared today.

When the silence concluded, Alan looked around at the smiling faces and felt grateful for the profound expressions of human spirit and connectedness. "Thank you all for being part of this gathering. You've shown me the power of transformation in our shared stories and reminded me that we are never alone in our journey toward renewal."

After everyone slowly began to disperse, Alan lingered for a moment in the clearing, letting the tranquillity seep into his bones. He felt an overwhelming sense of peace wash over him, a gentle reminder of the cyclical nature of existence—the constant ebb and flow of shedding and growing, fears and fears acknowledged.

As he walked back through the forest path toward home, he felt a familiar warmth unfurl within him—the serpent's energy coiled gracefully at the heart of his being, whispering reminders of the wisdom he carried. Each step forward was a pledge to honour both the light and the dark, acknowledging the duality of existence as he continued to evolve.

He had fully embraced his role not just as a psychiatrist or a mentor but as a lifelong learner, devoted to the art of transformation through experience. The work had only just begun; each day would present new opportunities for exploration, and he was prepared to embrace the multifaceted aspects of himself and those around him.

The following week, as they gathered for another workshop, Alan stood at the forefront, ready to guide them into new territories of discovery. There was a renewed vibrancy within him—an understanding that the path of transformation was endless, stretching far beyond the confines of his previous expectations. He could see not only the unique journeys of each participant before him but how they intertwined into a vibrant scenario of human experience.

"Welcome back, everyone," Alan began, standing in the sunlit clearing, his heart beating with anticipation.

"Today, I invite you to delve even deeper into the layers of transformation. Our focus will be on exploring the idea of nurturing our inner selves—the parts that may still feel fragile or unresolved."

A collective murmur of agreement rippled through the group as they settled onto the grass, finding comfortable spots in the circle. The energy was palpable as Alan prepared to guide them through a series of exercises designed to uncover hidden aspects of their identities that yearned for acknowledgment.

"Let's begin with a grounding exercise," he said, guiding them to close their eyes. "Take a deep breath and feel the earth beneath you. Visualize roots extending from your body into the ground, anchoring you firmly while also allowing energy to flow upwards." Alan demonstrated along with them, feeling the connection to the earth pulse with life.

As the group settled into the rhythm of their breaths, Alan facilitated the process with gentle prompts. "Now, as you breathe in, imagine drawing up energy from the earth—strength, support, and nurturing love. As you exhale, let go of anything that feels stagnant or burdensome. Release it back to the earth."

With each breath, Alan sensed the atmosphere around them shifting—a soft, healing energy enveloped the circle as participants embraced the practice, toying with the powerful imagery of release and renewal. He could feel their energy intertwining, a collective bond of understanding as they all shared in the experience.

"Now, I invite you to explore your inner landscape," he continued. "Picture yourself walking down a path in the forest, a path that represents your journey. As you walk, imagine yourself coming across different aspects of yourself—some that you recognize and cherish, and others that may feel unfamiliar or forgotten."

He watched as participants leaned into the visualization, their expressions transforming as they engaged with the imagery. Alan could sense the unearthing of emotions, the surfacing of memories, and the encounter with parts of themselves that had long been hidden.

"Allow whatever arises to simply be," he reminded them softly. "There is no judgment here—only acknowledgment. You can greet these aspects with curiosity and compassion."

He encouraged them to explore interactions with these parts, fostering dialogues between the familiar aspects they held dear and the neglected shadows that had lingered out of view. Alan took special care to remind them that within this exploration lay the potential for healing, understanding, and integration.

As they moved through the exercise, a gentle hum resonated within the circle—a harmony of hearts and minds working together to reclaim lost identities and nurture inner selves. Each participant responded differently, but the energy exuded a sense of openness and trust that defined their shared space.

After about twenty minutes, Alan began to guide them back. "When you're ready, gently return your awareness to the clearing. Wiggle your fingers and toes, bringing sensation back into your body. Open your eyes when it feels right for you."

As the group reconnected with the present moment, Alan noticed a newfound intensity in their expressions. The shared experience had deepened their understanding, creating a bond that felt almost sacred.

"To honour what we have uncovered, I invite you to share in pairs," he suggested. "Exchange what you discovered—the aspects of yourself you met along the path, what healing or insights emerged during this journey. Let's celebrate the multifaceted selves we embody."

Participants formed pairs, some speaking softly while others animatedly engaged in conversation. Alan moved among them, listening and offering gentle encouragement as he caught snippets of their discussions, which weaved together themes of hope, loss, and renewal.

When the sharing concluded, he called them back together in a circle. "Thank you for your courage in sharing your inner journeys," he said, warmth flooding his voice. "Today, we have uncovered not only fragments of ourselves but pieces of our collective experience, a testament to the richness that living fully entails."

To conclude the gathering, Alan proposed a ceremonial closing—an act that symbolized their commitment to nurturing the parts of themselves they had recently acknowledged. "Let's create a collective expression of our intentions for integration and healing."

He brought forth a bowl of water and a small basin, asking each participant to take a moment to reflect on a word, phrase, or symbol that represented their inner journey today. One by one, they dipped their hands into the water, whispering their intentions or affirmations, allowing the act of immersion to connect their words with the life force around them.

"I honour my curiosity," one participant said, allowing the water to spill through their fingers. "I choose to embrace uncertainty."

"I am reclaiming my voice," another declared, her hands cupping the water, holding her affirmations close before releasing them.

As each voice offered their intentions, the bowl filled with energy—the words dissolving into the water, mingling together in a beautiful dance of intention, setting the stage for a collaborative commitment to nurturing their growth. The collective energy of the group swelled, merging their aspirations into one fluid expression of shared transformation.

When the last participant had shared their intention, Alan felt a deep sense of gratitude wash over him. "Thank you all for your honesty and openness. As we release these intentions into the water, let's visualize them flowing out into the world, infusing our lives and the lives of others with the energy of healing and renewal."

With that, he gently lifted the basin and stepped toward the edge of the clearing where a small stream bubbled and flowed, its waters crystal clear and inviting. The group followed, creating a procession of intention toward the stream, their hearts aligned with each step.

Standing together at the water's edge, Alan held the basin, feeling the weight of the collective intentions resting within his hands. "As I pour our combined intentions into this stream, let's imagine them as seeds that will grow and flourish. Each intention becomes part of the greater cycle of life, nurturing not only ourselves but also the world around us."

He poured the water into the stream, watching it meld seamlessly with the current, carrying their hopes beyond the boundaries of the clearing. The stream sparkled with life, reflecting the glow of the sun overhead as it accepted their offerings, a reminder that their journeys were now intertwined with the flow of the universe.

"Let's take a moment of silence," he said, raising his hands in reverence. The group bowed their heads, creating a sacred container filled with the energy of gratitude, openness, and community. In that stillness, Alan felt the presence of the serpent as a guiding spirit, whispering the truths of transformation into his heart.

As the moment passed and they returned to the clearing, Alan sensed that their connections had deepened; they were not merely healing individually but collaboratively forming a vibrant community that could support each other through the complexities of life's transformations. A sense of belonging filled the air, binding them, and he could see it in their faces—a reflection of shared journeys and renewed hope.

"Before we end today's gathering," Alan announced, a smile stretching across his face, "I'd like to open the floor for any final thoughts or reflections on our experiences. How have today's exercises shaped your awareness of your inner selves?"

One by one, participants spoke, sharing insights and resonant feelings sparked by the day's events. Jasmine spoke of the beauty she found in vulnerability, proclaiming, "I've learned that it's okay to embrace my fragile parts. They don't diminish me; they add depth to the narrative of my life."

Liam expressed his excitement about the journey ahead. "Today inspired me to paint again. I want to create art that reflects not just my joy but also my struggles. Everyone has stories to tell, and I want to honour that."

The discussions flowed, laughter mingled with tears, and the spirit of transformation thrived in the clearing. Alan listened with an open heart, each story enhancing the collective fabric of their community, reminding him that each person's journey illuminated not only their paths but also the shadows of others.

When the time came to close, Alan gathered them in a circle once more. "Let us carry the energy we've cultivated today into the world," he urged lovingly. "Let's remember our intentions, nurture our journeys, and embrace the fullness of who we are—serpents shedding skins and emerging anew."

As they concluded the session with a communal embrace, Alan felt an overwhelming sense of fulfilment. He was witnessing the ripple effect of transformation, a testament to what could arise when individuals came together with openness and authenticity.

Back at his home that evening, Alan sat at his desk, the sun setting in a spectacular display of colours outside his window. He reflected on the day and how life had unfolded since he had first discovered the Amazonian mushrooms that catalysed his journey of transformation.

His thoughts drifted to the people he had met along the way, the stories that had been shared, and the healing that had transpired. The ripple effects of their transformations resonated within him, filling his heart with purpose and gratitude. He picked up his pen, inspired to continue writing—not just for himself but for those who shared in the ripple of connections they had forged together.

He wrote about the lessons learned, the cyclical nature of transformation, and the beautiful interplay of light and shadow. These were not just his truths but the truths of the countless individuals seeking their own metamorphoses. He felt compelled to capture this ongoing journey, a record of growth, healing, and interconnectedness.

In the months that followed, Alan's workshops and retreats continued to flourish, attracting participants from afar. They came seeking to explore their own narratives and the possibility of transformation. Through it all, he maintained a deep commitment to the principles that the serpent's wisdom had imparted—that embracing vulnerability and nurturing inner selves would lead to not only personal growth but also a profound sense of community and shared healing.

With each gathering, Alan noticed that his participants began to flourish, creating supportive friendships and networks that extended beyond the clearing and into their everyday lives. Many began to explore and share their art, their writings, and their stories, infusing their communities with the transformative energy they had cultivated together.

One particularly rainy Sunday afternoon, he hosted an open circle, inviting anyone from the community to attend—a space where both past participants and those new to the concept of transformation could come together. The atmosphere buzzed with anticipation as laughter blended with the gentle sound of rain pattering against the windows.

As the circle formed, Alan opened the floor by sharing a recent revelation he had experienced during one of his solitary walks in the forest. "Nature reminds us that we are part of a greater system," he began, his voice warm and inviting. "Much like the cycles of seasons, each of us faces moments of shedding and renewal. Today, I want us to explore how we can nurture our relationships with the earth and with ourselves as we navigate these cycles."

He guided them into a reflective meditation, encouraging everyone to close their eyes and feel the earth beneath them. "Imagine yourself as a tree, its roots deep in the ground, drawing strength and nourishment from the earth," Alan invited. "What does it feel like to be grounded and connected to the seasons of your life?"

As they immersed themselves in the imagery, he suggested they visualize how trees shed their leaves in autumn to conserve energy through winter, only to blossom anew in spring. "What parts of yourself can you let go of, in order to allow new growth?" he asked softly.

After several minutes, he encouraged participants to share their reflections. To his delight, hands went up excitedly as they took turns expressing their thoughts.

"I've been so burdened by my need for perfection in my work," a man named Marco confessed. "But now I see that I can take a step back, let go of that pressure, and allow myself to thrive in whatever form that takes—much like letting go of old leaves to make way for new growth."

Another participant, Elena, shared, "I've been holding onto guilt surrounding a relationship I ended. It feels heavy like a weight I carry. After today's exercise, I realize I can shed that guilt and open myself to healing and new connections. There's so much potential ahead of me."

Alan watched with appreciation as these moments of honesty unfolded—each voice adding not just personal reflections but communal strength. Their vulnerability became a source of empowerment, enriching the energy in the room.

As the conversations deepened, Alan suggested a new practice—working with vision boards as a collective manifestation of their aspirations. "Let's create visual representations of what we want to nurture in our lives," he proposed, leading them to a table filled with art supplies. "We can use images, colours, and words that resonate with our intentions."

Participants rallied around the materials, excitedly gathering images and crafting their vision boards. Alan moved among them, engaging in conversations and observing the creative energy in the air. There was laughter, shared stories, and moments of quiet reflection as individuals honed in on their aspirations—everything from career goals to restorative self-care practices.

Later, as they gathered once again in a circle to present their boards, Alan felt the atmosphere thrum with possibility. Each person eloquently articulated their visions: Marco spoke about pursuing creativity in his work artfully, while Elena expressed her intention to embrace love and connection in new relationships.

"Remember," Alan reminded them, "these boards are living documents. As we evolve, we can adjust and adapt our visions to reflect our journeys. There is no right way to grow; the process will always be unique."

As the sun began to set, casting a golden hue through the windows, a collective sense of hope blossomed among them. They had transformed a simple rainy day into a celebration of their aspirations and the shared commitment to nurturing themselves.

In the months that followed, Alan continued to weave these activities into his retreats, creating a platform for participants to share their visions, deepen their relationships, and learn how to navigate the complexities of their inner landscapes.

He also began to notice something awe-inspiring: many participants started to return to the clearing on their own to maintain the practice of self-nurturing and grounding. They formed friendships, created art, and supported each other's journeys, transitioning from attendees into leaders in their transformative processes.

One day, while preparing for a weekend retreat, Alan received a heartfelt letter from Sarah, thanking him for the profound influence he had on her life. In her letter, she revealed that she had taken her experiences from their time together and turned them into a community art project entitled "Shed and Bloom," where individuals could contribute their own stories of transformation through artistic expression.

"I wish to honour the journey we all share," she wrote. "And to create a space where others can explore their own paths of metamorphosis like we did. Thank you for showing me what is possible when we embrace our true selves."

As Alan read her words, he felt a swell of pride and joy bubbling within him. "Shed and Bloom" was a beautiful manifestation of everything they had cultivated together in the workshops—the spirit of transformation, community, and the courage to explore deeply held truths. He immediately recognized the profound impact that this initiative would have on their larger community, serving as both an expression of healing and a source of inspiration for those seeking growth.

He reached out to Sarah, expressing his enthusiasm for her project and offering to lend any support she might need. He suggested hosting a collaborative event at his next retreat, where participants could contribute their artwork and stories while engaging in discussions about their journeys of transformation. "Together, let's create a celebration that embodies the spirit of shedding and blooming," he proposed.

In the weeks that followed, excitement grew as details for the event began to take shape. Sarah coordinated a call for submissions, inviting individuals from the community to share their own stories and art. The response was overwhelming; people poured their hearts into their pieces—paintings, sculptures, poetry, and photography, each reflecting their unique experiences of transformation.

As the day of the "Shed and Bloom" celebration approached, Alan felt a palpable sense of anticipation. The clearing had become a sacred space of connection, and now it was ready to host not just their workshop participants but anyone else who wished to join in—to share their stories and witness the beauty that emerged when hearts opened.

On the day of the event, the forest came alive with energy. Lanterns hung from the trees, softly glowing as the sun set. The air was fragrant with fresh flowers, and laughter intertwined with the sound of nature, infusing the atmosphere with warmth and camaraderie. Participants gathered in small groups, sharing stories as they admired each other's artwork displayed throughout the space.

Alan stood at the centre of it all, his heart swelling as he walked among the participants. He was reminded of how far he had come—from a solitary scholar chasing the depths of his own consciousness to this vibrant community rich with shared experiences. He felt honoured to witness the richness of individual journeys folding into a collective narrative.

As the celebration commenced, he welcomed everyone to the clearing, a sense of unity enveloping them all. "Thank you for being here today," he began, his voice resonant and clear. "This is a space where our stories come together— where shedding our old selves allows for blooming anew. Each of you brings a unique presence, and today we celebrate the beauty in transformation."

He encouraged participants to take turns sharing their pieces, inviting vulnerability, and eliciting applause and support from the audience. Each story spoke of grappling with pain and fear, moments of surrender, and the rebirth that followed. Whether through a painted canvas hung on a tree or a poem recited aloud, the essence of transformation echoed throughout the gathering.

One participant shared a painting titled "From Ashes to Embers," depicting the slow process of rebirth from the depths of despair. "This piece represents my journey through grief," she explained, her voice a blend of pride and vulnerability. "From the ashes of loss to the hope that ignited within me. It's a reminder that beauty can emerge from even the darkest places."

Another participant, a young man named Amir, introduced his sculpture made from reclaimed wood. He spoke passionately about its significance: "This is called 'Roots,' and it symbolizes the resilience we build through our struggles. Just as this wood was once a living tree, we too have the power to adapt and thrive after being weathered by life."

As the stories continued to flow, Alan watched as connections deepened among participants. Individuals approached each other, sharing their experiences and finding comfort in knowing they were not alone on their journeys. In this space, the spirit of the serpent reigned—transformative, wise, and interconnected.

Toward the end of the evening, Alan invited everyone to come together in a circle. "Let's take a moment to honour the shared energy we've created today," he proposed. "This circle represents the strength found in community, acknowledging that each of us contributes to the greater scenario of life."

As they formed the circle, hands were held, creating a palpable connection that bridged each individual to the next. Alan led them through a guided reflection—encouraging them to express one word that captured what this celebration meant to them. "Speak your word aloud, and let it echo into our gathering."

Words like "resilience," "hope," "growth," "unity," and "rebirth" rose resonantly into the air as they passed around the circle. Each word became a thread woven through the scenario of their experiences, reinforcing the sense of community they had cultivated together.

As the evening drew to a close and the last remnants of daylight faded, Alan marvelled at how far each participant had come. He felt immeasurable gratitude for the lessons, connections, and transformations that had blossomed within the clearing—each heart like a flower unfurling petals

to reveal its vibrant colours, rich with potential.

As the final words were shared and the circle broke to embrace one another, Alan's heart swelled with joy. The "Shed and Bloom" celebration had encapsulated not just individual narratives but a profound collective journey toward resilience, healing, and renewal. Participants revelled in the energy of the moment, their interactions reflecting the very spirit of interconnectedness they had celebrated throughout the day.

As night enveloped the forest, they gathered around a large bonfire. The flickering flames danced amidst their laughter, creating a warm glow that seemed to infuse the air with magic. Alan watched as people shared stories, reminisced about their journey, and created new friendships that spanned beyond the boundaries of the clearing.

"Let's close our gathering with a ritual," Alan suggested, inspired by the energy around the fire. He invited everyone to reflect on what they would like to release and what they wished to carry forward. "In the spirit of shedding and blooming, tonight we will honour the parts of ourselves that we are letting go, as well as the intentions that we wish to nurture moving forward."

He provided each person with a small piece of biodegradable paper and a pencil. "Write down one thing you wish to release," he instructed. "It can be a fear, a doubt, or anything that weighs heavy on your heart. Once you've written it down, you can toss it into the fire, offering it back to the flames."

The participants took a moment to jot down their thoughts, some with furrowed brows as they wrestled with their burdens. Alan understood the weight of this exercise; letting go is seldom an easy act, but the warmth of the fire provided a comforting space to do so.

Once everyone was ready, he encouraged them to toss their papers into the flames, one by one. As each piece of paper touched the fire, a collective sigh of relief washed over them, accompanied by the bright crackling sound of the burning pages—a symbolic release of burdens into the cosmos.

"Feel the energy shift," he said gently, observing the way participants leaned in closer, faces illuminated by the firelight. "With these offerings, we are making space for what we want to cultivate in our lives."

After the release, Alan invited everyone to take another piece of paper and write down their intentions. "These intentions are seeds of growth, reminders of what we wish to nurture in our lives moving forward," he guided them.

As the participants wrote, murmurs of excitement filled the air as they thought about dreams yet to be pursued, passions waiting to be ignited, and connections they hoped to cultivate. Alan felt a resurgence of energy in the circle, sensing that their intentions were not just personal but woven into the very fabric of the community they had built together.

Once everyone had written their intentions, they went around the circle again, taking turns reading what they had crafted. Each declaration filled the space with warmth, a promise of personal growth intertwined with the commitment to support one another.

"I intend to embrace my creativity without fear," Jasmine declared, her voice carrying through the night.

"I will take steps to honour my mental health," Amir chimed in, empowered by the commitment to himself.

"And I will open my heart to new relationships," an older participant added, capturing the essence of the evening's themes.

As the intentions flowed, Alan felt the spirit of the serpent rising within the group, a source of guidance reminding them of the deep connection they each shared. This was what shedding and blooming looked like—a powerful acknowledgment of their multifaceted selves.

Finally, Alan led the group in a closing reflection. "Let us end our night by sealing these intentions with gratitude—for ourselves, for one another, and for the journeys we share. We are all in this together, surrounded by love and support as we navigate life's Challenges."

They gathered their hands once more in a circle, echoing previous sentiments of unity. As everyone expressed their gratitude, Alan felt a tear of joy swell in his eye. The night had become a beautiful celebration of the human experience—a scenario woven from threads of vulnerability, connection, and transformation.

In the days that followed, Alan found himself reflecting on the night's events. He was deeply moved by the growth he had witnessed among participants, seeing how the seeds of renewed hope had taken root through their shared experiences. The flame that had been lit in the clearing had sparked something far beyond one gathering; it was a beacon that illuminated their paths forward.

The "Shed and Bloom" project continued to expand; Sarah reached out to Alan with updates and ideas for workshops that combined art, storytelling, and healing. Inspired by the positive response, they collaborated on a series of events where both artists and community members could come together to share their work and cultivate creativity.

As the seasons began to change again, transforming the landscape into a scenario of vibrant autumn colours, Alan was reminded that transformation is ever-present. Whether through the shedding of leaves or the rich bounties of harvest, each moment was an opportunity for new growth and rejuvenation. The events of the past months had impacted him as much as they had the entire community, igniting a profound understanding of his role as both a leader and a lifelong learner on the path of transformation.

During one crisp autumn day, Alan prepared for the next workshop—a collaborative event with Sarah that would explore the intersections of art and healing. He arrived at the clearing, taking in the familiar surroundings, the air fragrant with the scent of fallen leaves. Under the backdrop of golden and crimson foliage, he arranged supplies for participants to create art reflecting their journeys and intentions.

When the attendees began to arrive, they greeted one another with warmth and excitement, the bonds forged in previous gatherings evident in their conversations. Alan welcomed everyone, feeling a deep sense of gratitude for the growth they had all experienced together. "Thank you for returning to this sacred space and for your willingness to engage in the transformative power of art and storytelling," he began, his voice steady and filled with warmth.

"Today, we'll explore how creativity can reflect the healing journey you've embarked upon. Remember that each piece you create is not just about the final product but the process itself. Allow the experience to be as profound as the art you create."

As they gathered their materials and began exploring different artistic mediums—painting, collage, and even poetry—Alan wandered through the clearing, offering encouragement and support. One woman named Claire was deeply focused on her canvas, meticulously layering colours as she articulated her journey through grief and resilience. "I want to express how beautiful the light can be even in the shadow of loss," she explained, her eyes shining with determination.

"This is a powerful vision," Alan noted, impressed by her insight. "Art can encapsulate the contradictory feelings we carry—both sorrow and joy coexist beautifully."

As discussions flowed, individuals shared their artistic processes and insights, creating an enriching environment ripe for creativity and healing. The atmosphere buzzed with laughter and connection as participants exchanged ideas, inspiration, and encouragement.

After several hours of pouring their hearts into their art, Alan called for everyone to take a moment to reflect on their creations. "What does your art reveal about your journey?" he asked. "What feelings or truths does it bring forth?"

As each person stood to share, it became evident that the act of creating had opened pathways for deeper self-understanding. Claire described her experience: "Painting helped me realize that even in my grief, there's beauty to be found. The darker colours represent the pain, but the highlights show the moments of hope that broke through."

Another participant, Marco, revealed his collage of photographs and words. "This represents my life's journey. The images I've pulled represent the moments I've cherished and the ones that Challenged me. Each piece contributes to the story of who I am today."

Alan felt a wave of emotions wash over him as he watched the vulnerability expressed in their words and art. It was a profound testament to the healing potential that art held—the ability to illuminate feelings that often reside in silence, waiting for a chance to be acknowledged.

The group shared their works in a supportive atmosphere, fostering feelings of validation and connection. Alan encouraged them to reflect on how their creations could serve as anchors—a reminder of the growth they had experienced and the transformations yet to come.

As the sun began to set, casting a warm golden light over the clearing, Alan felt a surge of gratitude for the beauty that had unfolded before him. He gathered everyone back to the centre and offered closing reflections. "Let's take a moment to honour the journeys we've shared today. Remember, as you leave, that your creations are reflections of your truth and can be a source of strength as you continue to navigate your paths."

With hands intertwined once again, the group shared one word (or phrase) that encapsulated their experiences of the day. "Hope," one participant spoke, followed by "Courage," "Resilience," and "Connection," each affirmation ringing through the air.

As they concluded, Alan extended his heartfelt thanks. "Thank you for your bravery in sharing both your art and your stories. You've brought light not only to your own journeys but to each other as well. May we continue to nurture these connections as we all blossom in our own unique ways."

As the participants began to depart, Alan stood back for a moment, letting the energy of the gathering wash over him. The clearing sparkled with remnants of their creativity—their laughter still echoing in the branches of the trees that surrounded them.

Reflections on the day swirled in his mind as he collected scattered materials and began packing his own art supplies. Each gathering had strengthened his resolve that fostering this supportive community was not simply a task, but a calling—a lifelong passion that brought him immense joy.

In the weeks that followed, Alan continued to facilitate events and workshops, each slightly different yet rooted in the same spirit of exploration and connection. The "Shed and Bloom" initiative flourished, merging art with discussions on mental health, mindfulness, and emotional resilience.

Inspired by the success, Alan reached out to Sarah and the other participants with an idea to mainstream their message of transformation beyond the confines of their forest gatherings. "What if we created an exhibition featuring our artwork and stories?" he proposed during one of their planning meetings. "It could serve not only to showcase the incredible creations we've all made but also to invite the broader community into our journey."

The idea sparked excitement among the group, and they quickly began brainstorming how to organize an event that would elevate their message of healing and transformation. They discussed venues, themes, and ways to engage the public in meaningful dialogue around the narratives that had emerged from their personal experiences.

As the participants united in this new endeavour, Alan gained fresh inspiration. He envisioned a vibrant exhibition not only displaying the art but also featuring interactive spaces for community members to engage in conversations, share their stories, and contribute their own art that reflected their journeys. This would be a celebration of resilience, a scenario woven from each thread of experience shared.

Over the subsequent weeks, preparations unfolded for what would become known as the "Shed and Bloom Exhibition." Alan, Sarah, and the participants poured their creativity into crafting an immersive experience. They designed interactive stations, live art demonstrations, and storytelling sessions where visitors could connect with the artists and the stories behind the pieces.

With the exhibition date approaching, excitement coursed through the community. Flyers were distributed, announcements made, and social media buzz cultivated a sense of anticipation among local residents about this unique opportunity to explore themes of transformation and healing.

On the day of the exhibition, the space was abuzz with energy. Alan arrived early to help set up, feeling a mix of excitement and nervousness. The venue was filled with artwork, each piece resonating deeply with the stories and experiences of those who had contributed. The air smelled of fresh paint, coffee, and the tantalizing scents of homemade treats contributed by the community.

As visitors began to trickle in, laughter and chatter filled the hall, creating a welcoming atmosphere as attendees exchanged greetings and marvelled at the artwork before them. Alan moved through the space, absorbing the positive energy and feeling the overwhelming sense of connection growing within the room.

The exhibition featured a large central mural, painted collaboratively by participants during one of their workshops. It depicted the journey of transformation, with vibrant colours representing the cycles of shedding and blooming. Surrounding it were smaller pieces, each with tags that told the stories of the artists—echoing the processes they had undertaken and the lessons learned.

As people mingled, Alan encouraged attendees to share their experiences with a provided prompt card: "What does transformation mean to you?" Many filled the walls with their thoughts, offering insights and reflections that deepened the collective scenario of experiences.

Attendees from all walks of life came together—some who had experienced their own transformations, some who were just beginning their journeys, and others who simply wanted to support the artists. Conversations flowed freely, much like the rivers in the forest, and Alan observed the beauty of human connection crystallize in real-time.

At one point during the exhibition, he noticed a young girl standing before a piece that depicted a phoenix rising from the ashes. Her eyes sparkled, reflecting a deep curiosity and wonder. Alan knelt beside her to ask, "What do you see in this artwork?"

"It's like the bird got hurt but then got better and flew up again," she replied, her voice bursting with innocence and excitement. "I want to be like that when I grow up!"

A smile crept across Alan's face. "That's a beautiful interpretation. We all soar after we've faced challenges. Each of us can rise, just like the phoenix."

As evening approached, a panel discussion was organized to delve deeper into themes of healing and transformation, featuring Alan, Sarah, and a couple of other participants. They shared their stories in an open conversation format, discussing the importance of community and creativity in their transformative journeys.

"It's through sharing our experiences, both the struggles and triumphs, that we gift one another the permission to explore our own paths," Alan stated. "We may find that the story we think is ours alone resonates deeply with someone else, and that connection is what fosters resilience."

After the animated discussion, the floor was opened for questions. Attendees appreciated the opportunity to engage, and insightful queries emerged about how to integrate creative practices into everyday life as a means of nurturing emotional well-being and processing challenges.

As the night wore on and the last of the visitors made their way through the exhibition, Alan felt a sense of fulfilments settle in his heart. The exhibition had become more than just a showcase of artwork; it had turned into a dynamic space of healing, a living testament to what could bloom when individuals came together with openness and intention.

As he packed the last items and prepared to leave, he joined Sarah and a few participants outside, where laughter echoed under the starry sky. Together, they shared stories of their favourite moments from the exhibition, buoyed by the success of their shared endeavours.

In that moment, Alan felt the timeless presence of the serpent within him—a reminder that transformation is an ongoing journey, marked by community connection and the courage to embrace both light and dark. The night sky shimmered with stars, mirroring the twinkling hopes and dreams that had ignited throughout their gathering.

"Tonight was incredible," Sarah exclaimed, her face aglow with excitement. "I never imagined our art and stories could resonate like this with so many people. It feels like we've really achieved something special."

Alan nodded, feeling a swirl of pride and gratitude for what they had built together. "It's a testament to the power of our collective stories. We've created a space where vulnerability can flourish—where healing can unfold in the shared embrace of community."

As the group chatted and reflected, Alan glanced around at the lingering participants, still animated and engaged with their thoughts and discussions. He felt a renewed commitment to nurturing this sense of connection. "This is just the beginning," he said, feeling the potential for what they could accomplish together. "Let's continue to explore avenues for collaboration, so more voices can be heard and more stories can be shared."

With unified determination, they began to brainstorm future events, excited about how to continue deepening their connections. The idea of art therapy workshops, storytelling circles, and even a series of nature retreats began to take shape, all grounded in the principles of healing and transformation they had embraced.

In the ensuing months, they launched new workshops and community events, each proceeding with the same spirit of inclusivity and exploration. Alan continued to lead discussions on the intersection of creativity, healing, and emotional resilience, combining insights from psychology with the powerful symbolism of the serpent—embodying the cyclical nature of existence.

Participants, inspired by their sense of community, even started to co-create their segments of workshops, offering their perspectives and experiences. The once solitary experience of healing transformed into an ongoing dialogue—a collaboration of voices that enriched the narrative of their lives and the lives of those around them.

As autumn gave way to winter, the clearing transformed once again, becoming a tranquil space of reflection. Alan invited the community to a winter retreat that centered around the themes of rest, renewal, and reflecting on their journeys. "Winter is a time of hibernation and contemplation," he explained in the invitations that went out. "Let's come together to reflect on our growth and care for ourselves as we prepare for the new year."

On the retreat, participants engaged in activities that celebrated rest, including guided meditations, journaling sessions, and quiet time in nature. Alan facilitated discussions on the importance of embracing stillness and using the winter months as an opportunity to look inward, shedding the remnants of the year gone by to make way for what lay ahead.

During the retreat, he encouraged participants to engage in small rituals that honoured their individual journeys. People created personal altars with organic materials found in the forest—stones representing strength, feathers symbolizing dreams, and leaves embodying transformation. Sharing these artifacts sparked deep conversations about aspirations and fears, reinforcing their sense of community.

One evening, as a swirling snowstorm blanketed the world outside, Alan gathered everyone around the warm glow of a fire crackling in the main lodge. The group settled in close, feeling the warmth wash over them.

"Tonight, let's share stories of our most profound moments and the lessons we've gained over this past year. We can each contribute to the fires of our stories, and in doing so, add warmth to our collective journey."

As participants spoke, their stories brought forth laughter, tears, and heartfelt reflections. A new mother shared her journey of embracing vulnerability through the chaos of parenthood, while a man spoke about reconnecting with his passion for music after years of self-doubt. Each narrative highlighted the power of transformation, reminding everyone that growth sometimes arose from unexpected sources.

As the last embers of fire flickered, Alan felt the weight of gratitude fill the room. The sense of intimacy forged through shared stories connected them all—their transformations not merely personal journeys but collective experiences woven together in a rich scenario of human existence.

The night wound down with a feeling of acceptance and peace, resonating within Alan and those around him. They departed the lodge, breathing in the crisp, cold air, staring up at the stars blanketing the winter sky. Each star felt like a reminder of the myriad pathways available—a celestial map guiding their journeys of shedding and blooming.

With the retreat coming to a close, Alan resolved to continue fostering these connections, remaining dedicated to the journeys each participant undertook. The spirit of transformation that had ignited among them was a flame that would not be extinguished; it was a collective fire; one they would fan together as they moved onward.

As they filed into their vehicles, ready to embark on their journeys back home, Alan felt a deep sense of belonging in the community of hearts that had gathered around him—people who understood and embraced the dance of shedding and becoming. Each person left with not just a commitment to their own growth, but an understanding that the cycles of metamorphosis

would continue to ripple through their lives long after they had parted ways. The shared laughter, pain, and insights formed a foundation that could withstand the trials of existence—a promise that they were never truly alone on their journeys.

As Alan drove home, the roads were slick with melting snow, evoking a serene sense of quiet that enveloped him. He felt a soft glow of contentment warming his heart, buoyed by the connections forged during the retreat and the collective spirit of transformation they had all engaged in. Yet, beneath that warmth, an undercurrent of exhaustion whispered reminders that he had been pouring himself into the needs of others for so long that he had barely taken time to nurture his own well-being.

Arriving at his home, he stepped into the study that had been his sanctuary through months of exploration and healing. The shelves were filled with beloved books, the desk scattered with sketches and notes from past workshops. He felt a sense of comfort and familiarity in the surroundings, but fatigue weighed heavily on him, pulling at his limbs and clouding his thoughts.

As he settled into his chair, leaning back momentarily to gather his resolve, he glanced out the window at the night's embrace. The moon hung high among the stars, illuminating the landscape in soft, ethereal light. It was a reminder of the beauty they all shared, the light that could emerge from even the darkest places.

But as he sat there, fatigue caught up with him like a tide, and suddenly the room began to spin. His breath quickened as a cold sweat formed on his brow. The weight of the past months—the emotional labour, the energies given, and the hearts tended—pressed down on him like an insurmountable burden.

He struggled to take in the comforting surroundings, but as the room blurred, the shadows grew heavier. Alan forced himself to stand, wanting to grab a glass of water, to somehow shake off the overwhelming sense of weariness. He pushed himself away from the desk, but his legs felt unsteady, as if they had lost their strength.

He staggered slightly, his vision narrowing, and instinctively reached for the edge of the desk in an attempt to steady himself. But before he could gather himself, the world spun wildly, engulfing him in darkness. The last sensation he experienced before collapsing was the cool surface of the floor meeting his body, an unexpected jolt before everything faded.

Time seemed to stretch infinitely in that darkness, a chasm where consciousness flickered weakly. He felt the weight of exhaustion seep into his bones, the weariness of a soul that had poured itself into countless journeys of others while neglecting its own needs. The paradox of guiding others through their transformations but having neglected his own echoed softly in his mind.

When Alan finally regained his awareness, he lay on the cold, wooden floor of his study, the quiet enveloping him like a heavy blanket. Panic briefly surged through him, but as he became aware of the stillness, he felt the warmth of the room wash over him. He realized with a sombre clarity that he had been running on empty—filling others' cups without tending to his own.

With great effort, he pushed himself to sit up, his body feeling heavy and unresponsive. He shivered from the cold of the floor but sensed a hint of clarity emerging— the reality that even the strongest must sometimes give in to vulnerability. There was beauty in being human, in recognizing the limits of one's energy, and what Alan needed was to pause, even if just for a moment.

As he sat there, bracing himself against the desk, staring outside at the moonlight filtering softly through the window, the reality of his situation settled around him.

.... *"All transformation begins with acknowledging where we are and what we need"*..........

That truth reverberated in his heart, and he allowed himself to understand that even the guide needed care, rest, and acceptance of his own limits.

With effort, he made his way to the chair and sunk into its familiar embrace, breathing deeply, trying to gather both his energy and clarity. He looked around at the sanctuary he had created—each book, each note, held wisdom that would continue to guide him—but he recognized that transformation wasn't just about the lessons of others; it was equally about honouring his own journey.

A heavy sigh escaped his lips as he felt the weight of fatigue settle in once more, but this time, it was accompanied not by shame or fear, but by the tender acceptance that should he choose to emerge from this moment, he could honour his own transformations just as fiercely as he had for those he guided. *The cycle was never-ending, and today, his journey was one of learning to embrace stillness and rest.*

And as the lingering shadows of exhaustion wrapped around him, he allowed himself to drift into a peaceful slumber, knowing that, like the serpent, he could shed this moment of vulnerability and arise renewed once more.

It was a reminder that every journey, no matter how transformative, must acknowledge both the light and the dark, the joy and the fatigue, for all were integral to the journey of existence. The seasons of life would continue to turn, and through each cycle, he would find the strength to rise anew.

In that quiet space, surrounded by the remnants of his work—artistic notes, unfinished manuscripts, and remnants of workshops—Alan drifted into sleep. The warmth of his retreat and the echoes of shared stories wrapped around him like a comforting embrace.

Hours passed, the moon arcane in its watch, its glow spilling gently into the room. The world outside remained hushed, blanketed in the calmness of winter, where everything lay still, waiting for the warmth of spring to reinvigorate life. Inside, however, Alan was a chrysalis—isolated yet imbued with the potential for renewal.

Eventually, a faint sound—a rustling in the hallway or perhaps a soft thump—stirred him. He blinked awake, gradually reacquainting himself with the familiar contours of the study. The light had dimmed further, casting long shadows across the floor. As the remnants of slumber ebbed away, reality washed over him, grounding him momentarily in the here and now.

Shaking off the fog of sleep, Alan remembered his fall, the disorienting sensation of overwhelm. He took a deep breath and recalled the lessons simmering in his unconscious: the importance of honouring oneself, of recognizing that the act of giving was futile if the wellspring ran dry. In that moment, he resolved to truly care for himself in the seasons to come.

Pushing himself to rise, he felt a lingering weariness in his limbs, yet there was a flicker of resolve igniting within him. This was not an end; it was simply a moment of pause—an opportunity to reflect on his journey. The realization washed over him that he had consistently nurtured others while neglecting his own need for rest and renewal.

He stumbled, leaning against the desk for support, and cast his gaze over the scraps of paper and notes scattered about. They told stories of transformation, healing, and connection—the very things he had sought to cultivate in others. But he also saw something else: a reminder of his own humanity, of the paths he had walked, the burdens he had breached, and the stories that still echoed within him.

Alan picked up a piece of paper, a poignant reflection from one of his past workshops that had resonated with his participants: *"To heal is to be whole, to love is to let go."* He felt the truth in those words settle deep within him, fuelling a sense of self-compassion and understanding.

After a moment, he moved slowly to a small shelf where he kept a few personal items—a small potted plant, a photograph of friends, and a stone with a word etched into its surface. "Breathe," the stone read—a gentle reminder he had lost sight of amidst the responsibilities he embraced.

He held the stone in his palm, feeling the weight of it, grounding himself in its presence. Breathe. The word resonated deeply; he realized that in the midst of guiding others, he had forgotten to tend to his own breath, his own soul.

As he prepared to settle into his make-shift bed in his lab, exhaustion tugging at his very being, Alan cast one last glance around the study. It was filled with everything he had created and cultivated—a sanctuary for healing, a place of growth. He vowed to return tomorrow with renewed purpose; he would take steps to prioritize self-care, honouring his own journey with the same dedication he offered to others.

With fatigue weighing heavily upon him once more, he slipped beneath the covers, surrendering to the soft embrace of sleep. As he finally closed his eyes, a gentle serenity enveloped him, bringing to the surface images of the community he cherished—the laughter, the stories of transformation, the beautiful scenario that had unfolded before him.

And as he drifted once more into the realm of dreams, Alan felt the light of the stars overhead—a reminder that even in the quiet, there resided an endless source of hope and possibility for what was yet to come. The serpent's wisdom whispered of new beginnings, and he embraced the sweet release into the stillness, knowing tomorrow would come with its own challenges and gifts—the cycles of shedding and blooming continuing on.

For tonight, he had allowed himself to pause, to reflect, and to commune with the subtle power of rest, affirming that even the most dedicated guides must, at times, embrace the vulnerability of being human.

In the solitude of his study, Alan fell into a profound sleep, a deep tranquillity that radiated through him like the first breath of spring after a long winter—an invitation to awaken anew, transformed once more.

Dr. Alan Pierce lay motionless, a twisted and serpentine creature, the dim glow of instruments casting shadows across his still form. The room, once vibrant with the energy of unceasing exploration, stood silent witness to the extraordinary conclusion of Alan's inner voyage.

For months, Alan had teetered on the brink, haunted by visions both beautiful and terrifying. The lines dividing his human consciousness from the serpent–like entity he had glimpsed became increasingly blurred. This merging of self-unleashed a tide of physical symptoms that eroded his strength yet brought him unexpected peace. Now, as he lay there, his body succumbing to the strains of traversing worlds, a profound tranquillity enveloped him.

In these final moments, as his breathing slowed and his pulse softened, Alan's consciousness danced on the edge of dissolution. The boundaries of self-unravelled gently, and his physical discomfort melted into a profound sense of unity and acceptance. The transition he had long contemplated was upon him, shifting from a theoretical endeavour to a tangible reality.

Alan's mind flickered with visions of snakes shedding their skin, juxtaposed with the human kindness and understanding he cherished. His dual identities harmonized, crafting a bittersweet farewell woven with the wisdom of a transformation attained.

Within this metaphysical union, Alan perceived the music of the cosmos—a symphony he had attuned to throughout his experiments. It resonated with the essence of his work—a delicate interplay of rational thought and untamed curiosity sculpted by a relentless yet compassionate seeker. This ultimate synchronicity unveiled the interconnectedness of all things, a profound gift as his consciousness gently merged with the universe.

Alan's physical departure was discovered quietly the next day by a colleague who had come to discuss their collaborative project. The sight of Alan's serene, relaxed body left an indelible impression, shrouding his life's work in a veil of mystery and reverence that lingered in the weeks and months following his passing.

Alan's office transformed into a place of pilgrimage for those who knew him, and even for those who had merely heard whispers of his ambitious and enigmatic research. His colleagues, surrounded by artifacts from his intense journey, marvelled at the expansive collection of notebooks—each meticulously detailing every experiment, abstract thought, and turbulent emotion. The sheer volume and depth illustrated a man both relentless and possessed, consumed by scientific rigor and exploratory transcendence.

His writings, interwoven with scientific diagrams and personal reflections, posed both a puzzle and narrative. Alan's intricate analyses were tempered with poetic musings on consciousness, portraying a man standing at the intersection of logic and emotion, of known and felt realities.

As the scientific community delved into Alan's legacy, discussions ignited. Sparks of intrigue and controversy intertwined with admiration and caution. His research, venturing beyond traditional boundaries, challenged ethical norms, prompting scientists, philosophers, and ethicists to debate its implications. Was Alan a visionary opening new vistas in understanding consciousness, or had personal obsession led him astray, eclipsing objective inquiry?

The debates extended beyond academic circles into broader society, where Alan's story took root as a cautionary tale of unchecked ambition. Headlines painted him as a scientific hero whose boldness mirrored ancient myths of overreach—his fate a testament to the delicate balance between discovery and hubris.

In academic institutions, Alan became an emblematic figure, praised for his courage yet critiqued for disregarding protective boundaries in scientific inquiry. His journey, forming the basis of public discourse and historical case studies, prompted new guidelines aimed at balancing innovation with ethical responsibility—emphasizing respect for the integrity of the individual psyche.

Amidst swirling debates, Alan's contributions to understanding consciousness glimmered brightly. The questions he posed, alive in the minds of his successors, nudged a new generation of thinkers toward pondering reality's fabric, telepathic connections, and the ethical structures governing such exploration. His synthesis of empirical data and speculative philosophy inspired interdisciplinary approaches, transcending conventional academic silos.

Thus, Alan's odyssey, marked by the pursuit of transformation and its repercussions, evolved beyond a cautionary tale. It served as a beacon pointing toward new horizons—an invitation for both risk and restraint, embodying the delicate balance of human endeavour where curiosity fuels advancement, tempered by ethical oversight.

Some perceived Alan's work as a roadmap to human consciousness's evolution, his insights offering glimpses into potential worlds untraveled. To them, Alan's life exemplified the imperative to break with tradition, transcending accepted boundaries to uncover truths veiled beneath conventional understanding—his intellectual daring a rallying cry for science intertwined with spiritual and philosophical quests.

Others regarded Alan's fate as an admonition—a reflection on the fragility of the human psyche and the cost of unrestricted exploration. These voices called for stringent ethical frameworks around experimental processes, particularly those influencing human consciousness's alteration.

Despite divergent views, consensus emerged that Alan's work expanded conversations on consciousness into new territories. Academia responded with heightened interdisciplinary collaboration, unravelling the complexities of the mind with collective wisdom from neuroscientists, philosophers, psychologists, and spiritual thinkers.

In lecture halls and conferences, Alan's name became synonymous with the pursuit of knowledge tempered by lessons garnered from his narrative. His journey inspired both fiction and non-fiction, depicting the tensions and tribulations of a mind not lost, but intrepidly chasing.

In this legacy, Alan stood as a figure of inspiration—a man reaching beyond his grasp with eyes wide open and a heart committed to understanding. His final metamorphosis resonated as an enduring reminder that in the quest to transcend, we must also seek integration, nurturing the length of human experience while exploring the heights of human potential. In this synthesis, the true harmony he sought—between serpent and man, consciousness and morality—awaited its rightful place in crafting a richly interconnected future.

In the wake of Alan's passing, the world he left behind was forever changed. His bold journey had not only reshaped the contours of scientific inquiry but also touched the lives and minds of those inspired by his daring pursuit.

Alan's colleagues, driven by a deep respect for his work and the mysteries he aimed to unravel, organized a symposium dedicated to examining the breadth of his research and its implications. Scientists, philosophers, and ethicists from around the globe gathered to explore the intricate scenario of Alan's findings, striving to reconcile the potential he saw with the risks he so boldly undertook.

At the event, diverse voices debated Alan's methods and the ethical boundaries he had questioned. For some, his blending of empirical evidence with philosophical inquiry symbolized a future where the limits of understanding were continually pushed further into uncharted territories. For others, it was a reminder of the need for caution—a balance between innovation and the moral responsibility that underpins all genuine scientific exploration.

Amid these discussions, one thing was clear: Alan's legacy transcended mere theoretical inquiry. He was not just a trailblazer in his field; he was a pioneer whose life illuminated the need for a harmonious blend of reason, compassion, and respect for the unknown. His work provoked a revaluation of how humanity approached the mysteries of consciousness, urging an embrace of both scientific rigor and spiritual depth.

The impact of Alan's work extended beyond academia. In the public sphere, his story captured the imagination of artists, writers, and creators who, inspired by his exploration, began to weave his narrative into their own forms of expression. Novels, films, and paintings emerged, capturing the essence of a man striving not just to understand the universe, but to find his place within it. Through art, Alan's journey continued to provoke questions about the future of human consciousness and the paths it might take.

As the years passed, Alan's influence only grew. His notebooks were preserved, not as mere relics of a scientific journey, but as maps guiding those who dared to follow. Students and scholars poured over his writings, using them as a springboard to explore new vistas, balancing innovation with the ethical frameworks Alan's life had impressed upon them.

In classrooms and laboratories, lectures and debates, Dr. Alan Pierce's presence remained vivid. His name became synonymous with a fearless pursuit of understanding, his life a testament to the profound truth that in seeking to transcend the known, we also delve deeper into the core of what it means to be human.

In the final echoes of his life, amidst the world he had strived to comprehend, Alan's spirit lingered, encouraging exploration tempered with humility, urging each new pioneer to question, to reach, and most importantly, to integrate. His legacy was a continuing journey—both a beacon of what might be and a gentle reminder of the beauty inherent in the world as it is.

And so, as the sun rose and set, casting its gentle light upon the earth, Alan's story soared into the great scenario of human endeavour. A constant whisper across the winds of time, inviting those who listened to ponder, to learn, and to dream.

RITUAL CLEANSING OF THE ANUNNAKI

- JOURNEY INTO THE GALACTIC REALM -

The ancient stone walls of St John's University, weathered yet enduring, echoed with the whispers of knowledge long pursued and cherished. They rose majestically around the vibrant campus, where students and faculty alike were drawn into the hum of academic exploration. Beneath the towering spires and between meticulously kept lawns lay the heart of discovery: the vast libraries and echoing halls that cradled the intellectual endeavours of the university's distinguished scholars. With their research journeys extending to the farthest reaches of human understanding, these scholars diligently worked to unravel mysteries across a broad spectrum of disciplines.

Amidst the shelves laden with heavy tomes and crowded archives, a new discovery had set the university abuzz—from its basement storage rooms to its sun-drenched, ivory-towered offices. This excitement revolved around the work of Dr Eleanor Carter, a remarkably talented postdoctoral scholar specialising in ancient scripts and civilisations in the Department of Archaeology. At just twenty-seven, Eleanor was already carving a niche for herself with her penchant for uncovering the links between ancient texts and historical mysteries. Her passion lay in piecing together forgotten stories from the scattered remnants of past cultures.

Dr Eleanor was a striking figure from a young age. The third child of Griffith and Bronwyn Llewelyn, she grew up on the rolling outskirts of Aberystwyth, a town deeply rooted in agriculture and renowned for its lush, sheep-dotted landscapes. This serene environment played a significant role in shaping Eleanor's inquisitive nature and thoughtful perspective on life. Even as a child, she often posed profound questions to her mother, like "Who am I? I seem to be asking this question as though I am standing outside like another person," revealing her early inclination towards introspection and philosophical pondering.

Her curiosity about the world extended beyond philosophical questions. A pivotal moment came during a school visit to Oxford University's Museum of Natural History. It was there she encountered the oldest skeleton of a modern human discovered in the UK, dating back 33,000 to 34,000 years. This encounter sparked her passion for archaeology, igniting a lifelong quest to unravel the mysteries of human evolution and consciousness.

Eleanor excelled academically and, after finishing her A-levels, secured a place at Oxford University with ease. Her time there was marked by an insatiable thirst for knowledge, culminating in a master's degree in Archaeology. Eager to delve deeper into her field, she pursued doctoral studies at St John's University, affiliated with Cambridge University. Her thesis, "Archaeological Dimension of Evolution of Human Consciousness from Archaic to Mythological Level," was met with admiration by her evaluators, earning her a prestigious postgraduate teaching and research position.

Dr Eleanor's research interests were wide and varied, yet she found herself particularly drawn to the transition from cave paintings to hieroglyphic symbolic language. This transformation symbolised a critical juncture in human consciousness and communication, reflecting humanity's evolving complexity and capacity for abstract thought. Her work not only advanced scholarly understanding but also illuminated the profound links between our ancient past and our present human experience. Through her studies, Dr Eleanor sought to bridge the gap between the archaic echoes of ancient art and the sophisticated narratives of today, driven by an enduring quest to answer the fundamental question of identity and existence.

Recently, Eleanor had succeeded in decoding an enigmatic clay tablet excavated from the ruins of Eridu, an ancient Sumerian city that thrived millennia ago in the fertile cradle of civilisation. This specific tablet was not merely an artefact; it held profound secrets woven into its ancient cuneiform impressions. The markings revealed a map of subterranean pathways, hinting at the existence of something extraordinary beneath the tunnels of Eridu's ziggurat—a landing platform for vehicles of the stars, in Sumerian mythology. Such an implication was enough to set Eleanor's pulse racing with equal parts excitement and disbelief. Here was a tantalising possibility: the prospect of an ancient civilization possessing knowledge of celestial travel, blending history with a hint of futuristic technology.

Dr Eleanor requested the services of Mark Reynolds, a renowned photographer in archaeological expeditions.

She met Mark and they preliminarily planned a detailed investigation.

As the rain drizzled softly against the windowpanes of the university's archaeology department in London, Dr Eleanor paced back and forth, her thoughts swirling like the grey clouds outside. Eridu awaited her — a scenario of ancient history intertwined with the remnants of a society long vanished. She glanced at the cryptic hieroglyph parchment, framed elegantly on her desk, the ink glimmering faintly under the fluorescent lights. It had arrived just weeks prior from the University of Chicago, an enigmatic artefact that had ignited her passion like nothing before.

"Can you believe this?" she exclaimed, her voice breaking through the quiet of the office. "Every pen stroke could be a clue; a key that unlocks the Sumerian world!" Her words were charged with a blend of excitement and urgency, a potent mix that seeped into the air around them.

Mark, her steadfast companion and investigating archaeological photographer, looked up from his camera equipment spread across the table. He flashed a grin that mirrored her enthusiasm. "It's not every day you get to travel halfway across the world to solve a mystery that could redefine Sumerian history! The contours in that parchment alone might have stories to tell."

Mark meticulously examined the camera settings; each click a reminder of the beauty he was determined to capture during their expedition. A seasoned photographer with an eye for detail, he relished the thought of preserving their journey—where every snapshot could be immortalised, etching their experiences into the annals of archaeological exploration.

"And you know," he added, his gaze fixed on the parchment, "the Eridu region is rich in archaeological wonders. If the hieroglyphs point to a specific location, who knows what else we might uncover? The thrill of discovery is intoxicating!"

Eleanor couldn't help but nod in agreement, her heart racing at the possibility. The hieroglyphs had suggested a linkage between Sumerian artefacts and ancient settlements in Hakkari. If they could decipher the meaning behind the cryptic symbols, it could lead them to a hidden narrative— one woven through centuries, waiting to be uncovered.

Their brushes with the past were not mere academic pursuits; they were intimate interactions with the lives of ancient peoples. Each twist and turn in the hieroglyphs resonated within Eleanor, connecting her to a time where Sumerian civilization thrived. The bustling ziggurats, the fervent scribes recording history on clay tablets— these visions brought to life her every aspiration. As a postdoctoral researcher, she had spent countless sleepless nights analysing texts and exploring the nuances of ancient scripts, but Hakkari felt like the pivotal chapter in her quest for knowledge.

"What do you think we'll find there?" she mused, her blue eyes sparkling with anticipation. "Do you think there could be undiscovered sites still hidden beneath the soil?"

Mark turned his camera toward her, clicking a shot that focused intently on her expression. "If history tells us anything, it's that the earth holds more secrets than we can fathom. Just imagine, Eleanor—it could be a small cave that we stumble upon, or a forgotten shrine. This is where the thrill lies; in the unknown."

His words hung in the air, creating a palpable tension—an excitement that thrummed just beneath the surface. Both shared a history of fieldwork that had seen its share of discoveries: crumbling tablets, ancient tools, and the residue of civilisations that spoke volumes through their silence. Each experience only deepened their desire to dig deeper into humanity's past.

Eleanor's discoveries, if validated, could straddle the realms of history and mythology, drawing lines that linked ancient ambition with modern scientific dreams. Eager to place her work under the auspice of academic scrutiny, she prepared to present her findings to the erudite minds at St John's University.

The grand lecture hall of St. John's, with its ornate wood-panelled walls and towering stained-glass windows, was a fitting venue for unfolding such momentous revelations. Scholars from myriad fields flocked to hear Eleanor speak, filling the hall with a hum of anticipation. As she articulated the significance of her work, weaving her scholarly insights with the suspense of discovery, the audience was spellbound. Among them sat Professor James Sinclair, a luminary in the field of astrobiology whose youthful face belied his breadth of knowledge and insight.

At 45, Professor Sinclair had already garnered significant acclaim for his pioneering research that delved into the origins of life beyond Earth. His explorations ventured into speculative realms of astrobiology, where he pondered the possibility of life seeded from distant worlds and the evolutionary potentials that lay beyond terrestrial boundaries. Sinclair's imagination was captured by Eleanor's findings, which seemed almost to echo his own scientific hypotheses with historical resonance.

He approached Eleanor after her presentation, the corridors still filled with the murmurs of inspired discourse. "You know," he said thoughtfully, his mind swirling with potentialities, "if there's even a grain of truth to what you've found, it could redefine our understanding of ancient technological capabilities."

Eleanor met his gaze, her eyes delighted by the idea of new collaboration. "That's what excites me—and frankly, baffles me—the most," she replied with a determined yet enthusiastic gleam. "I'm convinced that with the right expertise, we could unearth something revolutionary."

Thus, two inquisitive minds from different fields found common ground in the confluence of ancient scripts and astro-biological wonder—a partnership poised on the brink of uncovering a story that is ages in the making.

The interest of Professor Sinclair laid the groundwork for what would soon become a multi-disciplinary investigation at St. John's University, a place known for fostering pioneering research. The initial idea was to assemble a team that could both decipher and contextualise

Eleanor's archaeological find, yet it required someone adept at bridging the gap between ancient engineering and modern technology.

Enter Dr. Maya Thompson. At 41, head of the department of Propulsion Engineering, Maya stood out as a leading figure in aerospace engineering within the university's contemporary branches of study. Her work seamlessly blended the practical and the theoretical, exploring the deep roots of engineering principles as they evolved from ancient innovations to modern marvels. Her interest in historical technologies was not merely academic; she had published extensively on how ancient designs could inform and inspire today's technological advancements. The constructive collaboration promised by Maya's technical acumen and Eleanor's archaeological insights was ripe with the potential for groundbreaking discoveries.

This dedicated trio understood that they stood on the cusp of something extraordinary, yet they also knew that such an endeavour required the official endorsement and, crucially, the financial support of the university. With their preliminary team in place, they diligently drafted a comprehensive proposal for the University Senate. Their document detailed the interdisciplinary nature of their expedition and underscored the significant academic impact it could hold, weaving a narrative that connected archaeology, astrobiology, and aerospace engineering.

As the Senate convened to deliberate their proposal, the air was thick with anticipation. St. John's, an institution that prided itself on innovative research, recognised the potential of this venture—an unusual intersection of disciplines that promised not only academic enrichment but also the broadening of humanity's understanding of its past and its possibilities. However, the allocation of university funds demanded more than mere academic curiosity; it required the proposal to demonstrate concrete value and feasibility.

In a pivotal meeting, Professor Sinclair stood to present their case, his demeanour both earnest and electrifying. "Our investigation could redefine not only ancient history but modern science," he advocated. "If our ancestors had even the faintest grasp of space travel, we must explore how and learn why. This isn't just an exploration of ancient history—it's a glimpse into our shared human potential."

His impassioned plea, richly aided by Eleanor's thorough breakdown of archaeological elements and Maya's progressive technical insights, resonated with the Senate members. Added to this background, the rapid advances in AI and pioneering designs which companies like MDST (Multidimensional Space Transport) saw in this proposal the chance to support what could be transformative research, ultimately deciding to approve the initiative and provide funding to support the expedition.

As evening fell and the sun dipped below the ancient spires of St. John's University, the core team—Eleanor, Sinclair, and Maya—gathered in a small, softly lit conference room. Meticulously laid out before them were maps, diagrams, and Eleanor's decoded tablet. Their mission to

Eridu was a journey filled with promise, yet the complexity of the task called for further specialised support.

"We need to expand our team," Eleanor declared, her voice charged with determination. "Success hinges on more than just archaeology, astrobiology, and aerospace engineering."

Professor Sinclair nodded in agreement. "Precisely. We need expertise where we lack it. Medical support, navigation of geological challenges, precise documentation—all are crucial to our mission."

At this point in discussion, Eleanor pointed to her involvement with Mark Reynolds, and his eye for detail was very vital. It was agreed that Mark would be a natural choice to join the team.

Their second call was to Dr. Oliver Grant, a 42-year-old medical doctor whose calm demeanour in emergencies was legendary across the university. Eleanor approached him after a lecture on tropical diseases, reflecting his breadth of fieldwork experience.

"Oliver," she began candidly, "your expertise is essential to us. Navigating unknown terrains, your skills could mean the difference between minor scares and major issues."

Dr. Grant, intrigued by the blend of historical exploration and cosmic aspirations, accepted with a smile. "Keeping adventurers healthy while they chase historical whispers and cosmic dreams? Count me in."

The next day, Sinclair found himself heading for the bustling Earth Sciences building, seeking Dr. Richard "Rick" Morrison. At 45, Rick's expertise in seismology had made him a veteran of countless archaeological sites. His reputation for mapping the earth's invisible structures was unparalleled. He had led the team of experts in excavating overgrown pyramids in the thickly forested Mesoamerican region.

"Rick," Sinclair began, stepping into the office filled with geological maps and expedition mementos, "your skills would be instrumental. We need someone who can assess and navigate underground challenges and potential hazards."

Rick, captivated by the idea of delving into antiquity's mysteries through his scientific lens, was quick to join. "Helping unravel ancient mysteries one seismic reading at a time. I'm on board."

The atmosphere in the sombre, wood-panelled conference room of St. John's University was a mix of excitement and apprehension. With only a few weeks to go before setting off on their groundbreaking expedition, the team of six—Eleanor Carter, Professor James Sinclair, Dr. Maya Thompson, Dr. Oliver Grant, Dr. Richard Morrison, and Mark Reynolds—gathered for what they believed would be one of their many meetings on home soil.

Stacks of papers adorned the table: archaeological surveys, travel itineraries, lists of equipment. Mark's laptop was poised, ready to note any last-minute photographic requirements, and Rick was reviewing seismic maps for any indications of structural weaknesses in the ancient ruins they planned to explore.

The meeting room buzzed with the spirited conversation of scholars deeply engaged in planning the impending expedition. Maps rustled like whispers of ancient secrets, weaving a scenario of plans and possibilities.

Suddenly, the lights dimmed momentarily, and a shimmering holographic projection began to materialise in the centre of the room, halting all conversation.

This holographic figure, ethereal and enigmatic, seemed to be woven from the very fabric of legend. Hovering in mid-air, it exuded an aura of subtle authority. The projection's form was neither imposing nor diminutive, yet it carried a compelling dignity, as if born from the threads of myth and stars.

Adorned in attire that suggested a past rich with history and wonder, the hologram's patterns glimmered faintly in the room's ambient light, speaking silently of lost eras and distant places. Its eyes, although merely projections, seemed deep and soulful, looking beyond the physical to peer into the aspirations and dreams of those gathered.

In a silent symphony of light, the hologram approached Professor Sinclair. Each pixelated step echoed with a quiet power, drawing a virtual line through the hearts of the attendees. In its hand appeared a letter, bound with a holographic wax seal, an artefact of mystery and antiquity made anew in luminous pixels.

Professor Sinclair, entranced by the vision, reached out as the letter was digitally extended with a graceful motion, a ritual of trust transcending time. The seal bore an emblem foreign yet strangely familiar—a sigil- whispering the echoes of forgotten dreams, hinting at mysteries yet to be unlocked.

Accepting this virtual letter, Sinclair noted a name inscribed with elegant digital strokes: Ahniki. It was a name whispered in mythic circles, a figure of fable hovering at the boundary between legend and reality. The letter contained guidance and preparation instructions, crafted as though Ahniki himself had inscribed them from the echoes of time and destiny.

The holographic visitor offered a slight nod, acknowledging the gravity of his message, before gradually dissolving back into light and shadow, leaving the room enriched with a palpable sense of mystique—an imprint of his essence lingering in the air, promising revelations yet to unfold.

The door closed with a soft resolve, sealing the chamber back in reality but not without a shadow of that momentous visit.

It was as though an electric current pulsed through the room, the residue of the visitor's passage crackling in the silence now regained. Conversations slowly resumed, voices tentative and charged. Speculation buzzed around who the visitor might be, and what role Ahniki played in the unfolding events.

The room, though returned to its scholarly pursuits, carried an unmistakable shift in its fabric—a thread of myth woven into its ordinary weft. In the hours that followed, those present found themselves drawn deeper into the mystery, knowing that the visit, brief and wordless, had irrevocably set their course upon paths both wondrous and unknown.

Those gathered glanced at each other, a wordless understanding passing between them: this was no ordinary contribution. The envelope in Sinclair's hand might have been an artefact itself, containing insights or directives that could shape the very course of their expedition. Intrigue and a touch of the mystical now coloured their endeavour, leaving the team with a sense that their mission was destined for far greater significance than they had originally imagined.

"What is this?" Sinclair wondered aloud, inspecting the envelope. The seal was unusual, marked with an intricate emblem that none of them recognised: a mystical, intertwined design that seemed both ancient and curiously menacing.

"Open it," Eleanor urged, her scholarly intrigue piqued.

Sinclair carefully broke the aged, waxen seal and unfolded the letter, his brows furrowing deeper with each line his eyes traced. The paper seemed imbued with an essence not entirely of the modern world, carrying whispers from an era where myth and reality danced as one.

"I am Ahniki, I've heard of your expedition through the whispers of those who guard history's secrets, amplified by the earnest appeal and telepathic communication of Dr. Eleanor, synchronized in our Quantum communication channel" Sinclair read aloud, his voice imbued with a measured reverence. "We possess knowledge regarding your intended destination that transcends mortal perception. Only through a ritualistic cleansing, during the forthcoming winter solstice, shall the path be unveiled. This ceremony, six months, hence, will illuminate what has remained cloaked in the veils of antiquity."

Oliver, typically composed, seemed unsettled by the arcane suggestion. "Ritualistic cleansing? Is this some kind Voodoo stuff or a shaman incantation?"

Sinclair ventured further, his tone evolving from curious to intrigued with every word. "A condition accompanies this revelation: only two of your team's most worthy members may accompany me to bear witness to the unveiling, thereafter, guiding the larger group to decode the Ziggurat's mysteries and share this newfound wisdom with humanity. However, if you dare to unearth the true location and essence of the hieroglyphs on your clay tablet, you shall meet your demise. Thus, meet me on the outskirts of Hakkari, a location which will be revealed to you when you arrive at Hakkari. I await, your chosen two, in anticipation of their arrival."

A sombre and electrified silence enveloped the room, weighted by the cryptic invitation. The approaching winter eclipse, often enshrouded in human awe and superstition, was laden with significance for the team.

In Sumerian mythology, the winter solstice was associated with themes of death and rebirth. The Sumerians observed this period as a time when the sun god, Utu, appeared weakest, marking a transitional phase in nature's cycle. The solstice signified the turning point where darkness began to yield to light, symbolising hope and the eventual renewal of life. This cyclical pattern resonated with agricultural communities reliant on the shifting seasons for survival and prosperity.

Why the winter solstice may be because probably the weakened god Utu would not be able to guard the interplanetary portal or "Could this be a trap?" Rick posed, his pragmatic nature unperturbed by the allure of the mysterious.

"It resembles a riddle that demands our contemplation," Maya responded, her eyes alight with an almost fervent curiosity. "If it guides us to truly comprehend the mystery at hand, isn't the risk one worth taking?"

Eleanor, the youngest yet often the most incisive, pondered the letter's portent. "This straddles the boundary between myth and reality, merging the tangible with the otherworldly. Given the unique nature of these hieroglyphs and their historical imprint, perhaps such a ritual is indeed necessary to truly perceive them. The symbols seem to beckon understanding beyond mortal grasp."

The promise of uncovering something earth-shattering was intoxicating, even as the inherent risks loomed large. They debated who among them should embark on this enigmatic venture, aware of the delicate balance between caution and curiosity.

Their expedition, officially endorsed, began to take shape, a journey poised to transport them from the academic halls of Britain to the ancient spires of Sumer. All the while, the invitation to Hakkari hung in the air—an unwritten page promising to unravel secrets long thought lost to time.

Under the solemn gaze of St. John's venerable towers, the trio of Eleanor, Sinclair, and Maya embarked on preparations for their quest—a scholastic pilgrimage promising discoveries of a magnitude akin to those sung in ancient lore.

Selecting representatives for this mystical undertaking required not only physical resilience but a profound comprehension of their mission's scope. After deliberation, Eleanor stood as the natural choice; her unparalleled expertise with hieroglyphs and Sumerian mythology, honed through advanced AI data analysis, made her presence vital for deciphering any revelations.

Settling on the second participant proved more difficult. Oliver's medical prowess was essential to the main expedition's success; Maya, Sinclair, and Rick's specialised skills were likewise invaluable to the core mission.

Ultimately, at Eleanor's insistence, Mark Reynolds was the preferred choice. "Photography captures more than mere images—it seizes epiphanies. I can visually and conceptually document this journey, providing proof of what we encounter to confirm its authenticity."

Eleanor acknowledged his commitment to documentation and storytelling—qualities that might prove invaluable if the letter's promises bore fruit.

With this decision cemented, the team resumed their meticulous planning, integrating the cryptic sojourn to Hakkari into their itinerary. Eleanor immersed herself in tomes concerning ancient rituals, seeking insights that might illuminate their mystical path. Meanwhile, Maya and Rick explored how ancient seismic knowledge might entwine with their discoveries, preparing for what revelations might emerge through firsthand experience.

Meanwhile, Sinclair communicated the latest developments with university authorities, ensuring that funding allocations considered both the additional risks and potential groundbreaking outcomes this detour might hold. As they prepared, the group remained wary.

That evening, they finalised their plans. Their journey would take them from the bustling streets of London to the heart of Istanbul, and then onwards to Van—a route steeped in layers of history. Each destination called to them like songs from ages past. "We'll need to document everything," Eleanor reminded him, her voice tinged with urgency. "Every step we take in those lands will be a step closer to understanding the Sumerians' legacy. The Sumerians were masters of writing and art; we must capture all of it."

Mark nodded vigorously, more excited with every word she spoke. "And the locals! They might have insights we haven't even considered. Old stories can spark new ideas." He jotted notes, deciding he'd focus on gathering oral histories alongside their archaeological work.

As they packed their bags, Eleanor couldn't help but share stories of Sumer—tales of Ishtar, the goddess of love and war, and the stories etched in cuneiform that unfolded the lives of kings and commoners alike. The rhythm of her voice carried Mark farther into the imagery of the ancient lands they were about to explore.

Days passed, filled with last-minute preparations, deep dives into Sumerian manuscripts, and anxious conversations about their travels. The underlying excitement between them was contagious, an urgency that transcended the mundane. It spoke of adventure, of a shared passion that melded their two worlds—archaeological investigation and conservation. Mark, with his camera slung over his shoulder, was eager to capture the essence of this ancient land. He had always been drawn to the mystique of the Middle East, and the opportunity to document such a significant archaeological site was a dream come true.

Their journey began in London Heathrow, where they boarded a flight to Istanbul. From there, they planned to take another flight to Van.

As they set off from Istanbul, Eleanor and Mark were filled with a sense of anticipation. They knew their journey would be arduous, but they were determined to bring back a unique and valuable record of this lost civilisation which had advanced technology for space travel. The flight to Istanbul was smooth.

During their overnight stay in Istanbul, Eleanor and Mark found themselves in a hotel teeming with echoes of the past, much like the city itself. After a long day of travel and preparing for the next leg of their journey, they retreated to the antique-filled rooms. Despite their exhaustion, sleep proved elusive. Eleanor lay in bed wide awake, while Mark was blissfully asleep in his room. Eleanor listened to the soft murmurs of the Bosphorus breeze playing through slightly open windows when she noticed a faint light in the corner of her room.

Eleanor awoke to the distant, mournful wail of the wind sweeping through the narrow alleys of Istanbul, as if carrying the centuries-old secrets of the city right into her hotel room. The antique vase in the corner emanated a glow which seemed to materialise from nowhere, gently casting an ethereal light across an old vase adorned with Sumerian-like figures — a piece she hadn't seen before, seemed to pulse with a life of its own. She shivered, a sense of foreboding settling in her bones.

As the clock struck midnight, the atmosphere thickened with unseen energy. Suddenly, a spectral melody began to weave itself into the air, an ethereal song that seemed to emanate from nowhere and everywhere at once. Eleanor found herself drawn towards the sound; a hypnotic pull she couldn't resist. The song was unlike anything she'd ever heard—otherworldly, both beautiful and terrifying in its cadence. Slowly, the walls of her room transformed into a canvas for shimmering words, ominously recounting a decree from the ancient gods of the Anunnaki, condemning humanity to an unavoidable end.

Like the hand that wrote the message in the royal hall of Nebuchadnezzar, the apparition wrote the following words:

From high, the gods of Anunnaki speak,

Their whispers ride the winds of time's embrace,

Through veils of night, their voices subtly seek,

The minds of those who yearn to know their place.

To fragile Earth, where humans often stray,

Bound by the chains of ignorance and fear,

Understanding comes to those who find the way,

To pierce the shadows, see the vision clear.

In realms where intricate dimensions weave,

The Anunnaki secrets wait, profound,

Multidimensional words for those who believe,

And pure in thought, whose intents are sound.

Yet patience thins, as humanity falters, lost,

The cosmic echo warns of coming plight,

Where greed and sorrow exact their final cost,

And fading is the hope of endless night.

Beware the wrath of realms beyond mere sight,

Their stories carved in ancient starlight spun,

For only those who tread with hearts pure white,

May find redemption when all is said and done.

Thus, mankind's end, by choices long reaped,

Draws near as tales of warning now unfold,

Would that their wisdom finally be heeded deep,

As echoes of sorrow no longer leave hearts cold.

Eleanor felt the chill of despair seep into her heart, each note an echo of impending doom. As the music faded into silence, she was left trembling, haunted by a lingering sense of dread, and a traumatic awareness of irrevocable change.

The next morning, over breakfast, Eleanor described the night's mysterious events to Mark, who was enthralled yet sceptical. "Perhaps your mind is just attuning itself to the journey ahead," he suggested as they boarded their flight to Van.

Eleanor and Mark decided, at Mark's suggestion, that they stay in Van for two days to visit Akdamar Island situated in Lake Van.

It was already evening and after a good dinner and a night's rest, they planned to visit Akdamar Island. Mark was all excited as this tourist spot offered a great photo opportunity. They took the ferry to visit the church.

Mark gave a shout of exclamation mixed with fury as both his cameras were not recording any images. The attendant on the ferry, hearing the uproar Mark had created, approached him and made a poignant remark: "Sir, the church of the Holy Cross has miraculous powers and if you are not pure at heart, it will exhibit through subtle messages. I am a follower of Islam; I can sense the power of Shaitan."

Mark and Eleanor, being agnostic, dismissed the whole incident as unimportant. Yet, they both felt a little uneasy.

They decided to continue their journey to Hakkari.

They hired an air-conditioned van, comfortable for the long trip and to safely transport their equipment. Their van driver, also a local guide, was a man as enigmatic as the lands he navigated, led them along the winding roads. They politely enquired about the name of the driver and his mobile number, to call him when needed. He said his name was Suleman Erdal. A shiver went down the spine of both Eleanor and Mark as they subconsciously made a connection between Erdal and Eridu.

They called Erdal and told him to pick them up around 10:00 in the morning the next day after they had their breakfast, packed and ready. They now had a sumptuous dinner of Hünkârbeğendi, a delicacy of the Ottoman Empire, prepared with eggplant and turkey. They also indulged in a bottle of Kalecik Karasi, one of the best local wines. They retired to their rooms and immediately dropped off into deep sleep.

The journey from Van to Hakkari, a distance of slightly less than 200 Kilometres took them through a landscape both wild and beautiful, dotted with rolling hills and ancient fortresses. As they travelled, tales of ancient spirits guarding the mountain paths lingered in their minds, fuelled by the previous night's illusions and their experience in the lake.

Crossing into a particularly isolated stretch of road shrouded in dense fog, their jeep began to sputter. The guide murmured in frustration while attempting to coax the vehicle back to life, each mechanical cough echoing into the mist. As they waited, an unsettling quiet enveloped them.

Then, through the fog, they heard distant singing—an ethereal, mournful melody that resonated with a timeless essence. Both Eleanor and Mark exchanged bewildered glances as the song grew clearer, the cadence evoking images of forgotten rituals and celestial events, such as the soon-approaching winter solstice.

Determined to uncover the source, Mark quietly retrieved his camera, hoping to capture evidence of this spectral choir. He adjusted the settings to penetrate the mist, his lens focused on where the sound seemed strongest. However, the camera offered no answers—only silvery clouds danced across the frame.

Eleanor felt an overwhelming compulsion to listen and decipher the chorus as if the melody wove through her very soul, urging her to understand. As abruptly as it began, the singing faded, overtaken once more by the jeep's mechanical struggle to start. When the vehicle finally roared back to life, the silence lingered, enriched with a palpable anticipation.

These peculiar encounters left Eleanor and Mark with an unnerving certainty: they were truly on the edge of something extraordinary, where the veil between past and present grew thin. The echoes of some unseen force seemed determined to imprint their journey with an indelible message, promising revelations as profound and unfathomable as the long-buried secrets they sought beneath the ziggurat.

As the road unfurled towards Hakkari, Eleanor and Mark remained silent, their thoughts tangled in wonder and the fluttering uneasy certainty that something far greater than they anticipated waited on the horizon. They had booked two rooms in a hotel in the town centre. The date was 20th of December, and they felt that they could have well-rested sleep before embarking on the trip to Eridu in time for the rendezvous with Ahniki.

They had a sound sleep and were violently woken up by a loud knocking on the door. Their cab driver was standing there in front of Elenor's door. She wondered why he is still hanging around as they had settled his fare the previous night. The cab driver politely handed over a note to them in ancient parchment.

The parchment, very similar to the one which the messenger back at the university meeting room had handed over during their meeting at St. John conference room, had a cryptic message: "I am waiting for you in a vehicle outside the town and your cab driver has been intimated about its GPS location. Meet you soon."

The cab driver drove with an assured confidence as though he had some extraterrestrial understanding of the location. The darkness of dawn engulfed them and their cab stopped, and they could not see any sign of a vehicle when they slowed down some 20 miles outside the town limit. As their vehicle slowed down, they could see an intermittent flash of a small beam indicating the location of the vehicle. As soon as they got down carrying their luggage and standing in what seemed to be open countryside, their cab pulled away. After what seemed an eternity, a door opened on the side of the camper and Eleanor and Mark moved in with their luggage to board the camper. As soon as they entered with all their luggage, the van door shut and a regal voice came over a hidden speaker: "Welcome, my friends, Eleanor and Mark. The local time now is 7:00 p.m. and you can move to your quarters, which will be indicated to you by the lighted arrows on the alleyways. You can now have an eight-hour rest after you are refreshed and have had your dinner. You can join me for breakfast, subsequent to which we will embark on our journey to Eridu. That is where your ritual cleansing will begin.

I will talk to you again tomorrow morning. You can now watch the display console before you go into your quarters where the details regarding this vehicle will be displayed."

As Eleanor and Mark watched, their impression was one of great wonder. This was not a camper nor any ordinary vehicle. This vehicle combined innovative technology with modern comforts, redefining the idea of travel and accommodation. Eleanor and Mark eagerly read the display in wonderment like schoolchildren visiting a hi-tech exhibit.

"As you stroll to your chambers, I am an adaptive display who welcomes you to the realm of advanced technology transport—a marvel of futuristic design. Imagine the scene: the van's sleek, aerodynamic exterior captures your initial gaze, offering a glimpse into its innovative capabilities. Its shimmering surface is crafted from lightweight yet durable materials, promising not only safety but also an enhanced aesthetic allure. With its smooth, minimalist façade, it slices through air with ease, allowing for a seamless glide at a staggering six hundred kilometres per hour, all thanks to its groundbreaking magnetic levitation system. This system, a triumph of innovation, forgoes traditional wheels, enabling the vehicle to hover silently and vibration-free.

Picture its silhouette reminiscent of an enormous rugby ball, its colour subtly shifting, chameleon-like, to blend with its surroundings. Step inside, and the interior reveals itself as a haven of space efficiency and luxury. Your senses are greeted by a spacious living area, as adaptable as it is elegant, rivalling the comforts of a stationary home. The ultra-modern, modular furniture in your chambers transforms at the mere touch of a button—from a plush daytime seating arrangement to a fully extendable, cosy bed for the night. As the van's LED lighting system automatically adjusts, it creates the perfect ambiance to suit any occasion, whether it be a lively party or a serene evening retreat.

Imagine the culinary delights that await in the kitchen and dining area—a seamless blend of style and functionality. Innovative smart appliances, including a smart refrigerator, induction cooktop, and convection oven, make meal preparation a breeze. Surfaces are sleek and easy to maintain, matching the van's overall visual appeal. A retractable dining table emerges to welcome additional guests, while vast panoramic windows offer breathtaking views, turning each meal into a visually enriched experience bonded with the natural landscape.

As the journey winds down, find solace in the luxurious sleeping accommodations. Envision two fully equipped sleep pods, each featuring smart mattress technology that customises firmness, temperature, and sound for a restful, personalised night. Privacy is paramount, with soundproofing and programmable blinds ensuring an undisturbed retreat.

Further illustrating unparalleled ingenuity, experience the van's futuristic bathrooms. State-of-the-art water recycling systems and smart showers equipped with touch-free faucets and toilets bring modern convenience to new heights. Superior air purification systems guarantee a consistently fresh and pleasant atmosphere.

The entire journey is orchestrated in autopilot mode, the van expertly guided by sophisticated AI navigation. As it glides effortlessly to your desired destination, passengers can relax, knowing the van responds to voice commands, plans optimal routes, and even locates parking with ease. The robust wireless network ensures continuous connectivity, keeping passengers in touch with the digital world.

In essence, this extraordinary vehicle reaches the zenith of technological and design innovation, redefining the experience of the open road. It stands as a testament to luxury, sustainability, and advanced automation—a vehicle that feels as though it could ascend into the skies, transcending traditional travel and seamlessly merging with its environment.

For a moment, where time seems to have been compressed by a great magnitude, Eleanor and Mark stood rooted before the green glow of the display screen.

They then went to their respective rooms, and after a refreshing bath, they met for a light dinner. Their excitement in anticipation of what other wonders were in store for them led them to bed, where they almost immediately fell into a deep sleep. In the bed, the pillows on which they rested seemed to wrap around their heads. A peculiar calm pervaded their bodies.

While Eleanor, in her dream, found herself in a large study stacked up to the ceiling with ancient books, parchments, and scrolls. She had her photocopy of the Sumerian clay tablet spread out on a large black marble table. An apparition hovering behind her like a shadow told her in a baritone voice that what she was seeking lay beyond the domain of spacetime. Though she was able to read and translate most of the hieroglyphs, certain additional characters seemed to belong to something she could not classify. They did not appear to belong to the Sumerian, Egyptian, or Pali texts. She could understand that these symbols were only projections from another dimension.

As she racked her brain striving to decipher these unique codes, her internal alarm rang, and she woke up with a start. She had been asleep for exactly six hours. After freshening up, she went to Mark's room and knocked on the door. To her surprise, there was no response. She thought that perhaps Mark had overslept and proceeded to the living area. As she sat down on a comfortable sofa, she felt an overpowering presence and looked around.

The lounge of the camper van was filled with a cosy warmth, the dim light creating a comforting cocoon around Eleanor as she settled into the plush cushions. Outside, the world dimmed beneath the weight of twilight, but inside, the atmosphere thrummed with an expectant energy. She glanced around the small space, her heart racing with curiosity as the familiar objects took on an unusual aspect, coated in a veil of mystery.

The sound of the wind gently rustling the leaves outside was a soft backdrop, whispering secrets that tugged at her imagination. Each breath deepened her anticipation, the confines of the van both grounding her and igniting her spirit with the thrill of possibility. Eleanor felt as though she had crossed a threshold; this was no ordinary evening.

Suddenly, just past the reflection of the van's window, a shimmer caught her eye. She turned, her breath hitching in her throat as Ahniki appeared, seeming to materialise from the very fabric of the fading light. He stepped into the van with an ethereal fluidity, as if the barrier between the external world and this intimate space had dissolved.

His presence was both commanding and serene, infusing the camper with an aura that felt timeless and profound. The air around him shimmered subtly, as though reality itself bent to acknowledge the arrival of such a remarkable being. Eleanor felt a rush of warmth suffuse the small space, an awakening of the senses, as if the camper van had transformed into a sanctuary infused with magic.

As Ahniki's gaze met hers, it was as if a current of understanding passed between them, electrifying and true. In that moment, Eleanor understood that the van was not merely a vehicle; it had become a gateway to the extraordinary.

He did not need words to communicate; the silence between them was rich with meaning. Eleanor felt a warmth spreading through her, a reassurance that she was exactly where she needed to be. She sensed an invitation—a call to embark on a journey that promised discovery and transformation.

With a gentle nod, Ahniki acknowledged her presence and the courage it had taken for her to meet him. Then, almost imperceptibly, he extended his hand in a gesture both universal and intimate. Eleanor hesitated only for a heartbeat before reaching out, feeling the cool touch of his hand meeting hers.

In that connection, a flood of images washed over her—a scenario of visions filled with landscapes and faces, challenges, and triumphs yet to come. It was a glimpse into a future intertwined with purpose and destiny, hinting at paths she had yet to walk.

As suddenly as he had arrived, Ahniki stepped back, the moment lingering like the fading notes of a melody. Eleanor stood motionless, as though entranced, watching him disappear into the shadows that seemed to welcome him as an old friend. The grove returned to its familiar stillness, yet everything felt irrevocably changed.

In the quiet that followed, Eleanor was left with a sense of awe and a renewed spirit. The anticipation that had led her here was now a promise of adventure, and the wonderment of meeting Ahniki became a guiding light, illuminating the path that stretched before her.

Ahniki came down and sat on the opposite sofa. He cleared his throat and said, "Your friend, Mark, got cold feet at the last moment and he disembarked before we left Hakkari. Here is a note which he left by his bedside on the bedside tablet. It was transcribed to me last night, and I let him out of the vehicle and organised Erdal to drop him at Hakkari town centre."

Ahniki suggested that they have a light breakfast as the cleansing ritual, which he called a 'KTR – a Karmic Transformative Ritual,' would begin at exactly twelve noon. It was then that Eleanor realised that the day was the winter solstice.

Over breakfast, Ahniki explained that her ritual cleansing would be of a transformative nature as she was seeking knowledge in her evolutionary path towards higher consciousness, a superhuman. Ahniki took Eleanor to the control bay. The touch of a high level of technology was visible to Eleanor for the first time. Ahniki started the vehicle, and noiselessly it glided to a preprogrammed destination.

The vehicle stopped after exactly two hours, and they stepped out, and Ahniki declared that they were in the old settlement of Eridu. They were now facing a massive rock face covered in lush, thick foliage. Eleanor marvelled at the sheer natural beauty around them, but she was also aware that there was more to it than met the eye. Ahniki seemed unfazed by the seemingly impenetrable surface ahead. With practiced ease, Ahniki parted the tangled vines to reveal a smooth section of the rock.

Eleanor watched with curiosity as Ahniki retrieved a small, sleek device from his pocket. Its design was unlike anything she had seen before, smooth and metallic yet pulsating with a subtle energy. With a press of a button, the device emitted a narrow beam of light, intricately scanning the rock surface. The beam danced across the wall in a purposeful pattern, like an artist painting a masterpiece on a hidden canvas.

Without warning, a low rumble resonated through the ground beneath their feet. The rock face began to shift and shudder, revealing a perfectly smooth doorway emerging from what had once seemed an impenetrable mass. The entrance was just large enough to accommodate the vehicle that had brought them here.

As the door slid open, a faintly illuminated corridor extended into the mountain. Eleanor's anticipation grew alongside her sense of awe. The contrast between the natural beauty outside and the advanced technology within was stark.

They boarded the vehicle, and Ahniki guided the vehicle into the entrance, the soft hum of the engines echoing off the walls of the cavernous passage. As they journeyed further into the dimly lit space, Eleanor felt an enveloping sense of mystery and a promise of discovery. This was no ordinary path—it was a corridor to the unknown, a gateway to the possibilities that lay ahead.

After travelling a few hundred feet into the heart of the mountain, Eleanor and Ahniki came upon another door. This door was more discreet, with its seams barely visible along the rock walls. Ahniki, unfazed by their journey so far, produced the small device once again. However, this time, with a nuanced flick of his finger, a previously concealed compartment at the bottom of the device slid open, releasing another, more compact key. This smaller key, about an inch in length, was both delicate and robust—a masterful piece of engineering.

Ahniki placed his thumb on a recess on the key. A laser beam extended out of the key, and it started to configure as though enveloped by an invisible profile. The beam vibrated with a barely perceptible hum, and as it penetrated the keyhole on the door, the air filled with a faint, resonant chime. There was no turning of the key to unlock the door. The door, recognising the unique signal, unlocked with a subtle clunk and swung open silently, revealing a narrower passageway. When the passage door opened, another side panel closed shut on the side of the passage through which they had come, and their vehicle, as though on its own guidance, slid into the recess.

They stepped through this threshold. The corridor was like a technological conduit, about eight feet high and six feet wide, with its walls imbued with a gentle, diffused light that seemed to emanate from within the very walls themselves. The light bathed the passage in a serene glow, highlighting intricate patterns etched into the tubular surface—designs that pulsed softly, suggestive of some kind of bio-organic technology that was both advanced and aesthetically beautiful.

Walking through this corridor felt like treading a path suspended between worlds; it was modern yet almost mystical. As they reached the end of the passage, they entered a cylindrical chamber that unfolded before them with technological grandeur. The chamber towered above, reminiscent of the first stage of a space vehicle but constructed with such precision and transparency that each layer of its form appeared to float one within the other. The room's walls seemed alive, their transparency offering a window into the mechanisms and circuits flowing just beneath the surface.

Upon entering, the chamber filled with a soft, orange glow that diffused into the air, creating a warm and welcoming aura. The moment they stepped fully inside, the door behind them sealed seamlessly, leaving no trace of its existence. This encapsulated space was intimate yet expansive, designed to engage every sense.

From the smooth, reflective floor, a control panel began to rise, its surface streamlined yet dense with potential. The display was large, vibrant with graphs and readouts that reacted instantly to Ahniki's voice and touch command. At the control station, numerous holographic interfaces beckoned, each ready to respond to his touch or command.

Eleanor watched in awe, entranced by the harmony of technology and design. This was no mere control room; it was a nerve centre of possibilities, a place where boundaries dissolved, and the future was not just envisioned but executed. Ahniki approached the console, his fingers moving confidently over the controls, ready to unlock the secrets they had journeyed so far to uncover.

Ahniki paused for a moment, allowing Eleanor to absorb the weight of his words. The air in the teleportation chamber felt electrified with possibility, humming softly as if resonating with an age-old energy. He gestured toward the intricate designs that adorned the walls of the chamber, their luminescence pulsing rhythmically, like a heartbeat anticipating the next great leap.

"This chamber is not just a technological wonder; it's a bridge across time and space," Ahniki said, his voice steady yet imbued with reverence. "What we are about to embark on is a journey that transcends conventional travel. We are not merely going from one physical location to another; we're reconfiguring the very fabric of our consciousness."

Eleanor and Ahniki's transit would be akin to the teleportation of an energy capsule, transforming their very essence into a quantum-encrypted format. This advanced process would involve encapsulating their entire energy information within a sophisticated pod, resembling a polished sphere, meticulously designed to preserve and protect their identities.

Inside this sleek, shimmering sphere, their energy capsules would exist in a state of constant reflective mode, ensuring that every detail of their being is maintained without loss. The pod itself would harness a highly advanced warp drive system, allowing for near-instantaneous travel across vast distances.

As the warp drive activates, the energy capsule would dematerialise, streaming their quantum-encoded information through a complex network of spacetime. The entire transportation process would ensure that Eleanor and Ahniki remain intact, their consciousness wrapped in layers of encryption that protect them against external disturbances.

Upon reaching the desired destination, the system would reverse the process, seamlessly reconstructing their energy information through an entangled decryption. This innovative method of transit not only allows for swift movement but also guarantees the integrity of their identities during the journey, redefining the boundaries of travel.

He paused, letting that rich scenario of information sink in before continuing. "This journey to Alpha Centauri—a mere 4.5 light years away—will take only about eight hours because of this technology. We'll arrive at a destination unlike any you've ever known."

Eleanor's mind swirled with possibilities. The concept of warp drive had once belonged to the realm of science fiction, a fable spun by imaginative minds; now, it was a tangible reality that she was on the cusp of experiencing. "What awaits us there?" she asked, curiosity glistening in her eyes.

Ahniki smiled knowingly. "Our destination is an artificial planet situated in the Goldilocks zone of the Alpha Centauri system. It's called Nova Cognita. This place is a marvel—a thriving civilisation that has evolved over 50,000 years since its ancestors migrated there, thus escaping the great deluge at the end of the last ice age on Earth."

Eleanor couldn't help but be captivated by the idea of a civilisation that existed outside of Earth—a society that had survived the test of time and natural disaster. She imagined lush landscapes, civilisations blooming under alien stars, and cultures rich with history and knowledge.

"Your team at the university has already been informed of your long absence," Ahniki continued with a hint of urgency, sensing Eleanor's thirst for exploration. "They are prepared for your return; this mission is pivotal for everything you've worked on and dreamed about."

Eleanor absorbed his words as he initiated a sequence on the control panel, revealing a second layer of intricate data. "The launch pad for our journey is located at the apex of a Ziggurat structure, camouflaged against deep penetration radar to conceal it from prying eyes. The myriad technologies here have been designed to withstand even the most sophisticated surveillance methods. No one will know we've left."

As he spoke, Eleanor visualised the Ziggurat—an imposing edifice rising amidst the unassuming terrain, its angles and dimensions carefully sculpted to blend into the surroundings. Nature would have enveloped it in foliage, creating the illusion that it was nothing more than a natural monument.

"That sounds incredible," Eleanor said, her voice a whisper of awe. "What kind of civilisation exists there? What knowledge do they possess?"

Ahniki's demeanour shifted slightly; he appeared both proud and contemplative. "The inhabitants of Nova Cognita have developed a society steeped in an understanding of consciousness and energy. They specialise in harmonising the mind and body with the universe, having delved deeply into the realms of advanced biotechnology and energy manipulation. Their scholars have fostered wisdom that spans millennia, far beyond the grasp of contemporary science on Earth."

Eleanor's imagination painted vivid pictures of their advanced society—people coexisting with technology, living in elevated structures harmoniously interwoven with Nature's bounty. She envisioned lush gardens rippling with bioluminescent flora, energy sources harnessed from the very vibrations of the universe itself, and communities where knowledge was shared freely, guided by the principles of compassion and respect for all forms of life.

"The civilisation you will encounter is akin to what we might consider a utopia," Ahniki continued, as he activated a more intricate part of the holographic display. "The ecosystem of Nova Cognita, known as the 'Bio-Cybersphere', is designed to thrive without the constraints that traditional societies impose. They utilise advanced energy fields to create a sustainable environment, ensuring that their practices foster both advancement and ecological balance."

Ahniki's eyes sparked with fervour as he animatedly pointed to a rotating, three-dimensional model of the artificial planet. Floating cities spiralled upward from verdant valleys, each designed with organic forms that mimicked the natural world. In the skies above, ethereal constructs glimmered, resembling intricate webs interlinked with shimmering energy threads that pulsed rhythmically.

"They have created a symbiosis with their technology; it is an extension of their being, not a separate entity. Their mastery over natural energies allows them to perform acts we might deem miraculous—healing, environmental restoration, and the enhancement of physical and mental capabilities," he conveyed, his tone rising in excitement.

Eleanor listened, enraptured by the possibilities. "Will they be welcoming?" she asked, a hint of trepidation creeping in. "What if they view us as outsiders?"

Ahniki nodded reassuringly. "The beings of Nova Cognita are advanced not only technologically but philosophically. They have cultivated an understanding of the interconnectedness of all beings. Your presence as a representative of Earth—a conduit of knowledge—will be met with curiosity and open arms. They have much to share and, more importantly, much to learn from you as well."

Her heart raced as the significance of the mission sunk in. This was not merely a journey but a profound exchange of wisdom between worlds. "What will our days look like there?" she inquired, longing for a glimpse into her forthcoming life on this celestial sphere.

Ahniki smiled, his eyes glistening with shared vision. "Your time on Nova Cognita will be transformative. You will engage with their scholars, participate in communal experiences that blend science and spirituality, and deepen your understanding of consciousness itself. You will explore their vast libraries of knowledge, where texts are woven with the very energy fields that sustain their world."

With each word, Eleanor's anticipation swelled, and she could almost feel the rich scenario of experiences ahead. "How do we begin? How do we prepare for the teleportation?"

"First," Ahniki said, directing her attention back to the control panel, "we must configure our unique consciousness, the sum total of all information encoded both at the material and energy level, for the transition. The reconfiguration process will allow us to encapsulate all information contained in our current state. We will return to our original forms after our journey. It is vital that we approach this experience with an open mind, free of preconceived notions."

He activated a sequence on the panel, and a soft, melodic hum filled the chamber. "Once this process begins, you will feel a wave of tranquillity wash over you," he explained. "Your brainwaves will synchronise with the quantum fields, allowing for a seamless transition. When the time comes, simply relax and let go—trust in the process."

Eleanor took a deep breath, steadying herself. The grandeur of it all began to settle in—the weight of the knowledge she would acquire, the bonds she would form. "What about my research? My work?" she asked suddenly, only realising then how tethered she was to her life on Earth.

"Your work will be enriched beyond measure," Ahniki assured her, his gaze unwavering. "The insights you gain at Nova Cognita will provide new dimensions to your research. Knowledge from that world has the potential to transform not only your understanding but also that of your colleagues back on Earth. You will serve as a bridge, facilitating a dialogue that has been needed for eons."

Eleanor nodded, grappling with the profound implications of this journey. "All right, I'm ready," she declared, resolute. "Let's embark on this adventure."

Ahniki smiled warmly as he pressed a final series of commands into the control panel. "We will soon experience the wonders of a universe beyond our comprehension. Prepare for expansion, Eleanor. This journey will reshape not just your understanding but your very essence."

As the humming intensified, Eleanor felt her body begin to resonate with the energy around her. A cascade of gentle light enveloped them, swirling to wrap them in a cocoon of warmth and protection. She felt her consciousness expand, her thoughts cascading like water as they unravelled the boundaries of her being.

In one sweeping moment, the chamber fell away. Spaces and places flickered like fireflies, shimmering into existence and then fading as she transcended. What Ahniki did not disclose to Eleanor was that two complementary modules of information of their individual self would be generated. One would remain at a subterranean vault beneath the transponder and the other would be ferried to their destination. Using the concept of quantum entanglement, there would be a seamless transformation of information between the original and the complementary entities. Once the purpose of the mission is complete, the information module at Nova Cognita will be stored at a library. Both the information at the subterranean vault at the transponder and the library at Nova Cognita are maintained at near absolute zero temperature, like the one which is used for storing stem cells on Earth, but with the highest accuracy of maintaining a constant temperature close to absolute zero. This is the only way to store consciousness. It is essential that this temperature is much below the microwave background temperature to maintain the absolute integrity of the information capsules.

A welcome destination:

It was then Eleanor lost all sense of space-time, and she suddenly woke up from her bed in their hotel in Hakkari. She heard a loud knocking on her door and hurriedly wrapped her bathing gown around herself, rushed to the door, and opened it. Mark was standing there, looking as though he had seen a ghostly apparition. He then asked Eleanor to quickly get ready and join him for breakfast.

Seeing her confused look, Mark explained that it was 21st December, 11.00 in the morning, and that Eleanor had slept for more than 12 hours.

Still in a dazed state, Eleanor sat before her plate which was alluring with a selection of fruits and a separate plate of scrambled eggs. The silence was broken by Mark, who enthusiastically narrated his experience of the previous night.

A vivid memory of every detail of his dream. He was ferried on a surreal expedition to a higher-dimensional world. A realm where the air thrums with ancient energy and the sky shimmers with iridescent hues. Here, the landscape defies earthly logic, morphing with each step, as swirling mist envelops vast monoliths carved with cryptic hieroglyphs. Each symbol vibrates with stories untold, calling to Mark's photographer's instinct, urging him to immortalise their mysteries.

With every click of his camera's shutter, Mark anticipates capturing the essence of this enigmatic dimension. Yet, bewilderment cloaks his vision as the viewfinder presents not the otherworldly glyphs, but stark images of his own past. These spectral projections unfurl like a sinister slideshow, each frame unearthing deeply buried memories. Mark finds himself thrust back into the turmoil of his past life—a tumultuous relationship with a lover whose presence was as intoxicating as it was toxic. The viewfinder reveals tender moments twisted by betrayal, affection shadowed by discord, taunting him with scenes he longed to forget.

His heart pounds in rhythm with the relentless narrative unfolding before him, but the viewfinder refuses to relent, dragging him further into the labyrinth of his history. The dream morphs once more, and Mark, no longer the photographer, becomes a sombre sentinel of a grim chapter—his existence as a guard in a Nazi concentration camp. The air grows heavy with despair, as echoes of anguish reverberate in the distance. Mark witnesses the grotesque tableau of twisted bodies ensnared in a cruel barbed wire fence, their lifeless forms a testament to humanity's darkest extremes. Guilt clenches his heart like a vice, as he bears witness to the suffering etched forever in the annals of time.

In this higher-dimensional purgatory, Mark's soul trembles with a yearning for redemption—a wish to capture and understand not just the grotesque beauty of foreign realms, but the truths locked within his own fractured past. Yet, even as he reaches out, the hieroglyphic visions remain elusive, refracted through the prism of his conscience. The dream weaves a haunting narrative—not just of exploration, but a poignant journey into the recesses of guilt, love, and the indelible scars of memory. As the landscape folds in upon itself, enveloping Mark, he awakens with a start—his heart still racing, and his mind grappling with the kaleidoscopic collision of dimensions, both external and internal. He was totally soaked in sweat.

Mark immediately decided that this dream was an ominous warning as well as an indication to change his life's trajectory. He decided he would return to London and resign from all the activities where his motive was fame and wealth and dedicate his life to volunteering for the empowerment of downtrodden humanity. He quickly got ready, carrying only his laptop and backpack and leaving behind his cameras. He was ready to leave. It was then he realised that the day was winter solstice.

He realised that he had woken up from a nightmare and that Eleanor was still sleeping in the adjacent room.

Eleanor realised that she also had a dream in which great truth had been revealed.

They felt both exhilarated and grounded. Her dream had been a profound revelation, unveiling the layers of meaning she had long sought between ancient texts and the whispers of consciousness from Nova Cognita. The journey across dimensions was not just a physical voyage, but an exploration of the mind's vast potential—a symbol of humanity's possible evolution toward a heightened state of being.

Ahniki had guided her through a path of enlightenment that defied traditional boundaries, melding the essence of science and spirituality. The experience had deepened her understanding of consciousness, showing her that humanity could indeed aspire to new levels of awareness, much like the inhabitants of Nova Cognita. The vision of a society where technology complemented life seamlessly, fostering both personal and collective growth, lingered in her thoughts, urging her to embrace her own potential.

With Mark's decision to volunteer for an NGO, she saw the perfect constructive collaboration of change in both their lives. While he would capture the raw truth of humanity's struggles, she would delve into her research with renewed vigour, focusing on futuristic technologies that might one day help humanity transcend its current limitations.

Dr. Eleanor returned to St. John's University; her face serene but her spirit aflame with purpose. She walked through the hallowed halls, each step resonating with her newfound conviction. Though she shared not a word of her mystical journey, her colleagues sensed a transformation. Her dedication to researching the evolution of human consciousness through the lens of technology became her silent testament to the knowledge she had gained.

Simultaneously, in Sudan, Mark's presence as a photographer bore witness to the tragedies of war, capturing stories with empathy and truth. His work shed light on the plight of the voiceless, allowing their stories to inspire change. While their paths diverged, both Eleanor and Mark were bound by a shared purpose—a commitment to a world reaching patiently for its own Nova Cognita. In their hearts, they understood that the road to evolution was paved by both action and understanding, and they were ready to play their roles with courage and compassion.

As Eleanor immersed herself back into the academic life at St. John's, she embraced a quiet revolution. Her research into futuristic technology was driven by an urgent desire to bridge the gap between ancient wisdom and modern advancements. She envisioned technology not merely as tools for convenience, but as pathways for expanding human consciousness—possibilities she had glimpsed during her journey with Ahniki.

Her lectures began to reflect this shift. She spoke passionately about the potential of technology to enhance human understanding, using interdisciplinary approaches that combined archaeology, consciousness studies, and technological innovation. Her work inspired students and colleagues alike, planting seeds of curiosity and a thirst for exploration.

Eleanor's office became a bustling hub of activity, where ideas flowed as freely as the tea she brewed for her visitors. She built a team of like-minded individuals eager to delve into the mysteries of human potential. Together, they embarked on projects that explored everything from neural interfaces to enhancing cognitive abilities, pushing the boundaries of what was deemed possible.

Meanwhile, Mark's journey with the volunteer NGO took him to the heart of conflict zones in Sudan, where he found a renewed sense of purpose. The lens of his camera became a tool for advocacy, capturing not just the devastation of war but also the resilience and humanity of those affected by it. His photographs told stories that resonated with the world, stirring empathy and action among audiences far removed from the realities of the conflict.

Mark's work did more than document suffering; it highlighted the strength and dignity of communities, instilling hope that change was possible. He collaborated with writers, activists, and local leaders to develop narratives that called for global attention and intervention. For Mark, each frame was a step toward a more compassionate world, aligning with his new calling.

Though separated by geography, Eleanor and Mark stayed in touch, their correspondence a source of mutual inspiration. They shared insights and experiences, discussing the interconnectedness of their work—her scientific explorations and his humanitarian efforts. Each found in the other a constant reminder of their shared vision, that knowledge and empathy could change the world.

Their journeys, divergent yet parallel in their essence, reflected the potential for both personal and societal transformation. As Eleanor and Mark pursued their separate paths, they held in their hearts the profound revelations they had experienced together, carrying forward the light of Nova Cognita as a beacon for their lives and for the future they yearned to build.

www.ingramcontent.com/pod-product-compliance
Lightning Source LLC
Chambersburg PA
CBHW031552150726
47990CB00001B/315